HIDEOUT

Books by WATT KEY

Alabama Moon
Dirt Road Home
Fourmile
Terror at Bottle Creek
Hideout
Deep Water

HIDEOUT

WATT KEY

SQUARE
FISH

Farrar Straus Giroux
New York

SQUARE
FISH

An imprint of Macmillan Publishing Group, LLC
175 Fifth Avenue, New York, NY 10010
mackids.com

Our books may be purchased in bulk for promotional, educational, or business
use. Please contact your local bookseller or the Macmillan Corporate and
Premium Sales Department at (800) 221-7945 ext. 5442 or by e-mail at
MacmillanSpecialMarkets@macmillan.com.

Library of Congress Cataloging-in-Publication Data

Names: Key, Watt.
Title: Hideout / Watt Key.
Description: New York : Farrar Straus Giroux, 2017. | Summary: "The son of a
    Mississippi policeman finds a boy living in hiding in the wilderness and tries to
    help him without giving away his secret"—Provided by publisher.
Identifiers: LCCN 2016028002 (print) | LCCN 2016049828 (ebook) |
    ISBN 978-1-250-14397-6 (paperback)   ISBN 978-0-374-30483-6 (ebook)
Subjects: | CYAC: Mystery and detective stories. | Mississippi—Fiction. |
    BISAC: JUVENILE FICTION / Action & Adventure / General. | JUVENILE
    FICTION / Mysteries & Detective Stories. | JUVENILE FICTION / Law & Crime.
Classification: LCC PZ7.K516 Hi 2017 (print) | LCC PZ7.K516 (ebook) |
    DDC [Fic]—dc23
LC record available at https://lccn.loc.gov/2016028002

Originally published in the United States by Farrar Straus Giroux
First Square Fish edition, 2018
Book designed by Andrew Arnold
Square Fish logo designed by Filomena Tuosto

9   10   8

LEXILE: 630L

To Katherine Anderton because I owe you one

Special thanks to my helpful readers
Molly Kilpatrick and Margaret Davis

HIDEOUT

1

I SLOWED MY SKIFF AT THE MOUTH OF BLUFF
Creek and stared over the Pascagoula River. The far shore was
a looming wall of cypress trees and densely tangled underbrush
casting a long morning shadow over the black water. I set aside
my new fishing rod and pulled a map of Jackson County, Mississippi, from my pocket. I spread it on the seat and studied it.
The Pascagoula River Delta was a broad, uninhabited marsh,
indicated by a swath of green and hashed as wetlands. There
were no other markings on the map for miles except a few red
dots that I assumed were the old fishing camps. There were no
roads and no way into the place except by small boat. And
somewhere, in that enormous swamp, was a dead body.

Dad had mentioned the swamp to me a few times, sort of
like you'd talk about the moon. It was a place looked at from
a distance. A mysterious place one never imagines going to.

"I fished in the Delta once or twice with your granddad
when I was a kid," he said. "Back then you'd see people out
there. That was before the conservation groups bought up the
land and condemned the camps. It's easy to get lost. Cell

phones don't work. You get in a fix, and it's a long way to help."

I studied the river again. I had my flotation vest on in case I fell overboard or sank. I had a flare kit and a whistle in case I broke down. Dad is chief of police for Pascagoula, and he'd made sure I had every possible safety item. The only thing I didn't have was his permission to leave Bluff Creek.

He never actually *said* how far I could go. Considering I'd only gotten the boat a week before, on my twelfth birthday, and I wasn't the type of kid you'd expect to do foolish things, I doubt it crossed his mind that I would venture far from home. But I wasn't the kid I used to be. Even though school had been out for a while, the fight stayed over me like a blanket of sickness that seemed impossible to get out from under.

The school counselor told me I'd feel better over time, but I didn't believe him. When I talked to his calm face and tried to tell him what I was feeling, all I could think was that he couldn't possibly understand. Forget the physical pain—it was the humiliation that hurt the most. So I just started telling him and my parents what they wanted to hear.

That I was fine.

That I no longer thought about it.

Then the sessions stopped and I was left to figure it all out for myself.

There's not much to figure out. Trying to make friends in

a new town is already hard. Add getting beat senseless in front of the entire school, and things look hopeless.

For a couple of miles the river was nothing but a winding, featureless ditch of rich tannin-soaked water between cypress trees and savannas of tall buggy whips and marsh grass. Eventually I passed a creek that entered from my right; I remembered it from the map and kept going. From what I'd seen on the news, search and rescue, or S&R as Dad called it, had been mostly in the Ward Bayou Wildlife Management Area, still a few miles north of me. They'd found the abandoned jon boat sunk to the gunnels, streaked with blood, drifting slowly down the river.

As my outboard engine raced on, and home fell farther behind, fear swelled inside me. I came to a fork in the river, stopped, swallowed against the fear, and calmed myself. I pulled out the map again and located where I was. Just outside the management area. The right fork would take me directly into it.

There's no way you can get lost, I told myself. *It's just one fork in the river.*

I put away the map and sped up, forcing myself to press on. Now there wasn't even a distant cell tower or power line visible over the trees, making the river feel even more remote and empty. Maybe if I'd seen another boat along the way, I would have felt safer. Then I thought it was better that no one saw me. But mostly I thought it was the dumbest thing I'd ever done.

I soon came to another creek entering from the east. That was as far as I could make myself go. On the map it was called Ware Bayou.

I'll explore just this one. I won't even go deep into it. There's no way I can get lost after just two turns.

I motored into the mouth, and the cypress trees closed on both sides of me. They were seemingly taller, as if the swamp grew stronger the deeper into the heart of it a person went. Spanish moss hung from branches like the beards of old men. Beneath was a tangled thicket of palmettos and cane, swollen to an impenetrable wall of green with the wet June heat. The smell of the air was heavy and thick, like steamed vegetables. The foliage looked like a jungle, but I heard no bird or animal sounds. It was quiet and still. I heard nothing but my heart beating heavily in my chest and up into my ears.

As I motored slowly into the mouth the water cleared to a dark tea color. With the creek curving out of sight before me, I visualized the map, remembering the countless creeks and sloughs that in turn split off into more creeks and sloughs. A feeling of defeat settled over me as I contemplated what I was truly up against. This was just one of maybe a hundred waterways I'd have to explore. Unlike S&R, I didn't have a helicopter and night-vision scopes and real search vessels. It was going to be impossible to find a dead body in this place. Especially after everyone had already searched for five days and given up.

I looked down beside the boat, examining the dark-colored depths. I thought about the corpse rising up from the bottom, bloated and yellowish-looking like I'd seen in a horror movie.

What would I do if I found it?

Seeing it would be enough.

Then I'd report it. Then I'd be on the news and everyone would know about it. Dad would be so impressed with me that he wouldn't care that I'd taken my boat so far from home.

Suddenly the foot of my outboard motor slammed into something and shut off. Fear raced up my spine again as I spun and looked at the water behind me. I saw the tip of an old piling just inches beneath the surface. Dad called them deadheads, and the description had never sounded so fitting.

As I slowly drifted past the deadhead my mind flashed with visions of being stranded in such a place. Then something splashed to my left and startled me. I looked just in time to see an eight-foot-long alligator disappear into the depths. It seemed the place wasn't so empty and still after all. I imagined creatures of all sizes crouched within that green wall of tangle, watching me.

I stood up, grabbed the pull rope, and yanked. The engine

started, but I knew there was a chance I'd broken something. I put it into gear and let out a deep breath when my skiff started forward again.

It's okay, I thought to myself. *Just a little farther.*

I began seeing remains of the old fishing camps. A few were collapsed and partially sunken into the mud and hidden behind a screen of cane and vines and palmettos. Others had been burned and there was nothing left but the charred nubs of creosote pilings. It was like a strange ghost town. I passed eight of these eerie ruins before I came to one that was still standing. The roof was partially gone, and the deck looked too unstable to climb onto. On the outside wall was the number 34, sloppily spray-painted with blaze-orange paint.

I kept on, passing a few more of the abandoned camps, most of them barely visible, a few more with painted numbers, all of them looking too far gone to stay in or even fix up. More alligators slid into the depths. Occasionally a fish boiled the surface or a turtle scrambled off a log. A blue heron screeched like a banshee and glided away.

It wasn't long before I decided I'd gone far enough. Once I made this decision, I felt much more at ease and willing to pause and study my surroundings. I shut off the motor and drifted and listened. I felt safe in the middle of the creek, the sides of my boat protection from whatever lurked in my perimeter. There were more sounds I hadn't heard over the engine noise. An osprey cheeped from high in the branches of a bald cypress. Something croaked to my left. On my right the cane rustled and a tree branch shook and trembled. My eyes darted about, trying to catch a glimpse of the hidden creatures. I saw small birds flitting about in the underbrush. Then I heard another strange sound—hammering.

I turned my ear to the knocking. I determined it wasn't a woodpecker. It was someone hammering nails not far ahead of me. But I couldn't imagine what a person would be building this far in the middle of nowhere.

I started the engine again and eased forward, keeping my eyes on the creek bank ahead. As I came around the bend I saw another camp. It hadn't been burned, but it was leaning and rotten, and the door was missing. On the outside wall was the number 64. I studied the two front windows. Most of the panes were broken out, and the inside of the cabin was dark behind them. Then I felt the back of my neck tingle when I saw a ghostly image staring back at me, just above the window ledge.

2

BEHIND THAT WINDOW IN THE OLD CAMP WAS THE
face of a boy with crew-cut hair and glasses. I lifted my hand
off the tiller and gave him a weak wave. The boy waved back,
then disappeared. After a moment he stepped onto the rickety-
looking deck that fronted the house, holding a hammer. He
appeared to be close to my age, but a little on the small side.
He was barefoot, filthy dirty, and his clothes were torn in
several places. His face and arms were dotted with so many
insect bites it looked like he had chicken pox. He adjusted his
glasses and studied me.

"Hey," he called.

"Hey," I called back.

"What you doin' out here?" he asked me.

"Nothing," I said.

He kept staring at me.

"Where'd you come from?" I asked.

He pointed to a place beside the camp. "I paddled that boat."

I saw the outline of a canoe almost completely hidden in
the marsh grass.

"The canoe?"

"Yeah. You gonna tell anybody?"

I shook my head. "No."

He smiled. I felt myself relaxing, mostly convinced I wasn't talking to a ghost.

"I like your boat," he said.

"Thanks."

"You wanna come see my camp?"

I thought about it. "Okay," I finally said.

I motored over to what was left of a narrow boat dock. Most of the boards were gone. The boy came across the front deck like there wasn't anything wrong with it, stepping over rotten places and open holes and down onto the dock to help me. I met him at the front of the boat and gave him my bowline. He took it and wrapped it around a nail.

"I need a cleat," he said, meaning a metal hook to fasten boat ropes to.

I thought it strange he would think of something minor like that.

I stepped carefully onto the dock and looked back at my boat to make sure it wasn't floating too close to any debris that might scratch it.

"It'll be okay," the boy said, like he knew what I was thinking.

I turned to him. "I didn't know people could have camps out here anymore."

"Yeah, they told my brother it was fine."

"Who told him?"

The boy shrugged. "I don't know. Whatever person he asked. This used to be our camp about five years ago. Before the government took it away."

"You build it?"

"Daddy and my brother did. I wasn't old enough. But I used to come stay in it with 'em."

"You're lucky it didn't get burned like those others."

He turned and admired the dilapidated old structure. "I know. I've been tryin' to get the orange paint off. Come see the rest."

I followed him up the dock and onto the deck, stepping carefully in his footsteps.

"What's your name?" I asked him.

"Davey," he said. "What's yours?"

"Sam Ford," I said.

We stepped into the camp and I looked about the dark room. It was no more than sixteen feet wide and twelve feet deep. It was definitely leaning, but inside it wasn't as noticeable. The roof had obviously been leaking for a while. The plywood floor, damp and stained, flexed under my feet. The place smelled of rotting wood and animal pee. Against the wall was a bunk bed. The mattresses had holes on the sides where rats had torn into them and pulled out the stuffing. To my left was a countertop with a sink and old dishes and a coffee-maker. An old charcoal grill sat on the floor.

"It won't take me long," Davey said. "I swept most of it out already. I just need some wood."

"Where's your dad and your brother?"

"They're comin'," he said.

"How long have you been out here?"

"About a week."

"By yourself?"

"Sort of. I have a mouse. You wanna see?"

Davey went to the counter, where there was a rusty cooking pot. He looked into it, then held it out to me. I peered in and saw a ball of what looked like mattress stuffing.

"Feel in there," he said.

I didn't like the idea of poking my finger into a mouse nest. "Will it bite?"

"It's just a baby," Davey said. "I was cleanin' and I messed up its nest. The momma ran off."

I nudged the nest and saw a hairless pink mouse baby. Its eyes were closed and it was no bigger than the tip of my thumb. The mouse squirmed at the disturbance and worked its way back into the stuffing.

"I named him Baldy," Davey said.

I replaced the stuffing over Baldy and backed away.

"What do you and Baldy eat?" I asked.

"Well, we need some more food. And some boards."

"You don't have any food?"

"I caught some fish. And I found three cans of beans in the cabinet under the sink."

"What are you drinking?"

"Dr Pepper. We left it up here."

"You mean, like, five years ago?"

"Yeah, I guess."

I watched him, thinking maybe this was all a joke he was playing. He didn't appear to be joking at all.

I had so many questions I didn't know where to start. "When are your dad and brother getting here?"

"I don't know. Soon."

"Like today or tomorrow or what?"

"I don't know."

"But all you have is a canoe. What if they don't come for a week?"

Davey adjusted his glasses. "They should be here by then, for sure," he said.

"How can you stay here without any food?" I said. "You don't even have bedding or anything, and it looks like a thousand mosquitoes have bitten you."

"They're gonna bring everything I need."

"But you need it now."

Davey smiled and grabbed a broom leaning against the wall. He made a couple of sweeps across the floor and smiled. "They'll come," he said. "Real soon."

It was almost eleven o'clock and I needed to get back in time for lunch. Just an hour before, I would have sworn I'd never venture into the swamp again, but now there was something irresistible about this strange boy and his swamp camp.

I got some insect repellent out of the tackle box in my boat and brought it to him. "You can have this," I said.

"Thanks," he said.

"I'll bring some food," I told him. "But I have to go home first and check in with my parents."

"What about some cheese for Baldy?"

"You think Baldy's big enough for cheese?"

"I don't know. What do you think?"

"Milk, I'd say."

Davey watched me expectantly as I got back into my boat.

"I'll try and bring some," I said.

He smiled like it was something he couldn't help, excitement rising into his eyes.

"Can you spend the night?" he asked.

"My parents wouldn't let me," I said. "I'm not even supposed to be this far away from our house."

A little of the excitement faded from his face, but the smile stayed.

"But I'll bring you a sleeping bag. Okay?"

"Okay," he said.

Davey shoved my boat off and I backed away from the dock. He gave a small wave. "See you this afternoon."

3

I IDLED OUT OF THE CREEK, CAREFUL NOT TO HIT a submerged tree or another deadhead. Once I reached the river I sped up again and steered toward home. It took me twenty minutes to get back to Bluff Creek, where I made a wide turn off the Pascagoula and slowed the boat. Then I was no longer worried about making it back in time or getting stranded in the swamp.

A little ways up the creek I turned again into Kings Bayou, a mile-long waterway lined with waterfront homes. I lived almost at the end of the bayou, where the land was lower and the houses less expensive. On my left, at the mouth of the bayou, the ground was higher and the homes nicer. All of the docks were roofed, with decorative patio furniture on the deck and expensive motorboats in the lifts. Grover Middleton lived on the point in the nicest house of them all. As exciting as my experience had been that morning, thoughts of the fight crept into my head again and smothered it away.

Grover, I'd come to believe, was the cause of my problems. If we'd never met, the fight wouldn't have happened.

I'd been doing a lot of thinking about just how I'd come to be his friend. On the surface it was obvious. When Dad got his new job as chief of police last September we moved down from McComb. Grover was the first boy I met. I ended up talking to him when we had doughnuts in the fellowship hall after church service. Even had I not been eager to meet some kids my age, he would have been hard to ignore. He's got wild, kinky red hair that sits on his head like an Annie wig. There's no way to brush it or do anything with it except let it grow and shear it like a sheep. Contrasting this is skin so fair it looks like he would get sunburned just crossing a parking lot.

Our friendship was even easier when I found out he was in my same grade at Gautier Middle School and happened to live just down the bayou from the brand-new house we had moved into just two months earlier. I liked video games, and he knew more about them than anyone I'd ever met. So we started hanging out at my new school, and eventually I started going over to his house on weekends. There probably wasn't a single boy our age who could have walked into Grover's house and not been envious. Dr. Middleton was a surgeon at the big hospital in Pascagoula, and he bought Grover anything he wanted. He had remote control planes and guns and fishing rods and two iPads and a MacBook. He even had a boat, a brand-new Boston Whaler that he'd never used. But I soon found that, despite having everything a kid could want, all Grover really cared about was his Xbox.

So it appeared obvious how we'd gotten to be friends. But what bothered me was that I never saw any of this coming. How did I not know that everybody thought Grover was so lame? How could I start off in a new town as the best friend of the biggest chump in school?

Counselors and parents just tell you whatever they can to make you feel better. It appeared to me that I was just as big a loser as Grover. And it took getting beat within an inch of my life to realize it.

I think of it as "the fight" in my head, but only because it sounds better. There was no fight to it. Grover and I didn't do anything but lie on the cold cement and ball up and cover our faces while they kicked us until I thought I was going to die.

I'd told Dad and the other policeman what had happened at least ten times. I'd replayed it in my head a thousand times more, trying to make sense of it.

It happened right after we returned from Christmas break. We were leaving the lunchroom when Leroy Parnell stuck out his foot and tripped Grover. Leroy was a full ten inches taller and twice as heavy as either one of us, with size twelve shoes and a tear tattoo just below his left eye. He was in eighth grade, but I heard he'd been held back at least two years.

Grover's backpack was always so overloaded and heavy that he smacked hard onto the concrete. Grover's got a quick temper when something stands in his way. I saw his face growing red, and I knew he was about to lose it. He finally untangled himself from his backpack, got to his feet again, and turned to Leroy.

"Watch it, dumbass!" he shouted.

Grover's not scared of anything, but not in a brave way. He can be so unaware of his surroundings that he doesn't even consider what's dangerous and what's not. I knew Leroy was no one to shout at. No one to even talk to. And I knew he'd tripped Grover on purpose.

Leroy leaned down close to Grover's face and said, "Do something about it, wuss?"

Grover doesn't care about people calling him names. It's like he's above that kind of thing, like he doesn't even hear it. But he *hates* people getting in his face.

"Why don't you pick my bag up for me, you stupid redneck!" Grover shouted.

Standing beside Leroy was his friend Gooch. Nobody knew Gooch's last name. Gooch never said much. He had homemade tattoos of a chain around both wrists.

Leroy looked at Gooch like he was about to ask him something. But the look was really more like *You see, I told you he'd act like this*. Then, while Leroy was still looking at Gooch, his arm shot out and his fist punched Grover in the chest so hard it sounded like a hammer thumping a wood barrel. Grover flew backward into the lockers and collapsed onto the concrete walkway. I started to go to him when I felt Gooch's arm slide around my throat and constrict me in the crook of his elbow. I heard Grover wheezing and trying to catch his breath. As I felt my own breath being cut off I saw Leroy approach Grover and stand over him for a moment. Then he kicked him in the stomach and bounced him off the lockers like a soccer ball. Grover's body made a huge bang, and I realized other students were starting to gather around. Out of all the faces the one most in focus was Julia's. She appeared frozen with her mouth open, watching in disbelief. She was the prettiest girl in our class and the last one I wanted to see this.

I felt fear and panic surge through me like I'd never felt before. I began to struggle against Gooch, trying to break free. Then I felt a sharp blow to my ribs, and what breath I had left me and everything went blurry. I heard Julia scream. I felt Gooch's arm loosen, and I slipped to my knees on the concrete. Things were getting louder around me. More people were screaming and yelling. Gooch kicked me in the stomach, lifting my backpack and the rest of me off the concrete. I came down on my face like I'd been slapped with a brick wall. I don't remember much after that except the screaming and yelling. It seemed like the beating wasn't ever going to stop. Blows to my face and stomach and arms until it didn't hurt anymore. And I thought, *This is what it feels like before you die.*

I woke up in the hospital with Dad and Mom standing over me. I learned the police, including my dad, had locked down the school while they pursued Leroy and Gooch, who had run off across the soccer field. While the ambulances took me and Grover to the hospital, the officers tracked them down in the woods and arrested them.

Later on, I saw Grover in the hospital room a couple of doors down. He had a brace on his nose and bruises all over his body. Leroy and Gooch got expelled and transferred to a juvenile detention center. The rumor around school was that they'd done it all on a bet.

Why me? I kept asking myself.

I'm not the smallest in the class. I'm actually a little on the tall side, but skinny. I play on the basketball team, even though I'm not very good. I'm not one of the smartest in my grade, but I'm usually in a couple of advanced classes. I'm not outstanding in any way. I doubt that many people even knew my name before the fight.

So why me?

"Those boys are not just bullies," Dad said. "They're criminals. I imagine both of them will live in jail most of their lives."

That didn't help.

"Sam," Mom said, "it was a terrible thing that happened, but you have to know it had nothing to do with you."

That didn't help either.

I heard that, while we were in the hospital, Principal Hartley held a schoolwide assembly about bullying. He said there was a zero-tolerance policy about it and he'd put a letter box outside the main office for students to make anonymous reports.

It makes things even worse to have the entire school make an example of you.

Most of all, it's an empty, dark feeling when you realize adults can't fix everything. Just like the counselor, they were going to tell me what I wanted to hear, anything they thought would make me feel better. Which isn't always the truth. But even the truth doesn't always fix things.

I got beat up because Leroy and Gooch thought I was a loser and I wouldn't fight back and people would think it was funny. And with friends like Grover, I figured, I'd always be a loser.

4

WHEN I RETURNED TO THE HOUSE I FOUND DAD ON
the dock in his black police uniform. His shirt collar is deco-
rated with stars, and his badge glinted in the sun. He wears
a utility belt that weighs nearly ten pounds, with his 9mm
Glock pistol, two sets of handcuffs, Taser, and flashlight. As
if the badge and the belt weren't enough to scare a criminal,
his arms are nearly as big around as my leg and his muscles
strain against his shirtsleeves.

Dad's project of the day was wiring the engine on the new
boat lift for the *Bream Chaser*. That's what Dad had named
my boat. I think it was his attempt at making a joke, a bream
being a small perchlike fish. Since the fight, he'd been making more jokes and I figured it was his way of gauging my
enthusiasm. Outside of his occasional not-funny jokes, Dad's
pretty serious. He's always thinking about work and projects,
but even more so since we'd moved to Kings Bayou.

Dad's originally from Bay St. Louis, a coastal town not far
west of Pascagoula. He grew up fishing and boating the Gulf
of Mexico with his friends and my grandfather. While we

were living in McComb and he was still a sergeant, all he talked about was moving south again. Then he got the new job at the end of last summer. Being chief of a police department was the goal he'd been working toward since the academy. As soon as we moved he bought a waterfront lot on the bayou and began building his dream house. The construction workers had finished in March, and we'd been living in it for almost four months.

I tied the *Bream Chaser* to the dock, trying to remember the knot Dad had taught me.

"Catch anything?" he called out.

"No, sir," I said. I knew he was watching me fumble with the rope. The knot is called a bowline. It's supposedly the best knot in the world. It looks easy when he makes it, but I only get it right half the time.

"Make a loop," he said. "Then the rabbit comes out of the hole and around the tree."

I fumbled it again.

Dad walked over and knelt beside me. "You just gotta make your rabbit hole the right way," he said.

He made his first loop and quickly pushed the rope end out of the hole, around the stupid tree, and back down the hole, cinching the knot tight.

"Takes a little practice," he said.

I didn't see how it was possible to learn everything he knew, but I wanted to try.

"I'm going inside to get something to eat," I said.

I walked up the dock and into the house and saw Mom in the kitchen putting a corned beef into the Crock-Pot.

"How was it?" she asked me.

"Fine," I said. "But I didn't catch anything."

"Are you hungry?"

"Yes, ma'am."

"This corned beef won't be ready until supper, but you can grab a snack to tide you over."

"Sounds good," I said. "I'm going to put my stuff away."

"Grover left two messages for you on the answering machine."

"Okay," I said. "Thanks."

The television in my room was full of Xbox messages from Grover. The good thing about him never using his boat was that he couldn't come after me. But I doubted he even realized I was avoiding him. Things like that didn't seem to register with Grover.

Where are you?
Call me.
Something wrong with your stinking phone?

Ignoring Grover's communication attempts just annoyed him and made him pound out his messages in all capital letters.

I turned away from the screen and flopped onto my bed. I lay there and stared at the blades of the ceiling fan and got my head back into the adventure I'd had that morning. First I thought about Davey and how strange it was that he was out there by himself. Then I thought about the dead body and how ridiculous it was to think I could find it. Davey and the swamp camp were suddenly more interesting than the dead body. But the more I thought about it, the more Davey's story didn't sit right with me. There were a lot of pieces missing. The mystery of it was enticing, but I also couldn't think of ever doing something that made me feel so different.

The Xbox chirped.

ANSWER ME!

I grabbed my backpack off the floor and returned to the kitchen. Mom had gone onto the sun porch to touch up one of her paintings. She used to work as a legal secretary when we lived in McComb. She was always coming home late and dumping stacks of take-home work on the kitchen counter. She said as soon as she and Dad saved up enough money for the move to Pascagoula she was going to find less stressful work and take up painting again, something she'd enjoyed in college. She works part-time as the secretary at our church now, and when she's not working she spends a lot of her free time creating oil paintings of the water and the wildlife outside the window. She doesn't sell them, but to me they look as good as anything you'd see in a gallery. I was sort of surprised by how good they were, but Mom's like that. It seems like she's quietly good at everything.

Mom had left out a sandwich for me and I stuffed it down. Then I put my backpack on the counter and began to fill it. I got three cans of ravioli, two cans of corned beef hash, two bananas, a bag of potato chips, four hot dogs, and several slices of cheese. Then I filled an empty milk jug with water and set it on the counter beside the pack. Finally, I filled an empty pill bottle with milk and put it in a Ziploc bag with an eyedropper Mom used to use to give me medicine.

A sleeping bag was going to be a problem. There was no way I could get one into my pack and it was probably too hot for one anyway. I decided to take two old bedsheets instead. It was enough to give Davey a little comfort and to block mosquitoes until his family arrived.

Just as I was about to go out the back door I heard the phone ringing.

"Can you get that, Sam?" Mom called from the sun porch. "It's probably Grover again."

"Okay," I said with a groan.

I went into the kitchen, put everything on the floor, and picked up the handset.

"Hello," I said.

"Why haven't you been communicating with me?" Grover said. He was always impatient but even more so on the phone.

"Because I've been too busy to play Xbox."

"Busy doing what?"

"I've been in the boat."

"Why?"

"I've been fishing."

"Why?"

"I don't know, Grover. Because sometimes people go fishing."

"What's the point in it?"

"It's just fun."

"You never liked to fish before."

"Yes I did. Dad just hasn't had much time to take me."

"What about me?"

"Geez, Grover. It's only been like a day since I was online."

"Well, you have a lot of catching up to do. I'm at level three on Demon Quest."

"I'll catch up."

"When?"

"Tomorrow, I guess."

"Come over after church. We can stay up late."

I looked at the floor. It was easy to avoid Grover in my head, but it was much harder to avoid him face-to-face, or ear to ear in this case.

"Okay," I said, feeling like a coward. "Are you going?"

I hadn't seen him at church in weeks, and I assumed his mother had been traveling. Dr. Middleton didn't attend service, and I never saw Grover there unless his mother took him.

"Yeah, I'll be there," Grover said, like it was a dumb question.

"All right, then," I said.

"Good," he said. "See you tomorrow."

The phone clicked and went silent.

Dad was still working on the boat lift at the end of the dock. He straightened and eyed my backpack.

"Getting serious about fishing, I see."

"I guess. Mostly exploring."

"You'll get the hang of it. Look for structure along the bank, and fish against it. Before you know it, you'll drag a big redfish out of there."

"I'll try."

He studied me, beaming. It was obvious that he liked nothing more than to see me enjoying the boat. It was just the type of outdoor thing he thought I should be doing.

"You show Grover your boat yet?" he said.

"He doesn't care about that kind of thing."

"Maybe he just doesn't know what he's missing. I'll bet some pretty girls would love to go riding with you two."

I thought of Julia in my boat. I imagined her sitting on the front seat and looking back at me with that smile and that blond hair blowing about her face.

I frowned. "I doubt it."

"You might be surprised," he said.

He wasn't even close to understanding.

"I haven't been hanging out with Grover as much lately."

I studied Dad's face, searching for some sign of approval, but his expression didn't change.

"Why not?" he said.

"I don't know. I'm just not into the Xbox as much, I guess. That's all he likes to do."

I'm not sure what Dad thinks of Grover. Like everybody else I know, he probably just can't imagine how you connect with him.

Dad turned back to the lift. "I think you'd be doing him a favor to stop off and get him out of the house some."

"I'll see him at church tomorrow."

"Suit yourself," Dad said. "Have a good time."

I got into the *Bream Chaser* with my backpack, started the engine, and sped away toward the strange world of the swamp and Davey. Where, if even for just a little while, I didn't have to worry about who I was and who I hung out with.

5

DAVEY MUST HAVE HEARD MY BOAT APPROACHING, because he was already standing on the dock when I rounded the bend. I tossed him the rope, he tied it to the nail, and I got out with my pack and water.

"I thought you might not come back," he said.

"Take this stuff," I told him. "I've got to cast at least once."

"Did you get milk?"

"Yep."

He took the pack and water from me while I got my fishing rod.

"There's a lot of fish out there," he said.

I made a cast, reeled the line back in, and returned the rod to the floor of the boat.

"You got to try more than that," he said.

I climbed back onto the dock.

"I told Dad I was going fishing. So now I have. You hungry?"

Davey nodded. "But I need to feed Baldy first."

"Dump the stuff out of the backpack," I said.

Davey dumped the contents onto the deck, and I picked up the Ziploc bag with the milk and dropper. I gave it to him, and we went inside the camp and stood over the pot that held Baldy's nest. Davey seemed to know what to do and took some milk into the dropper, dug around until he found Baldy, and dripped some on the mouse's face.

"Doesn't look like he's drinkin' it," he said.

"Put it in his mouth."

Davey tapped Baldy's mouth with the tip of the dropper. After a moment the mouse mouthed at it and appeared to take some of the milk.

"How much you think?" Davey asked.

"I don't know anything about it," I said.

Baldy took a few more drops, then refused to open his mouth.

"Maybe you should try again later," I said.

Davey studied Baldy for a moment, then put the dropper into the bag again and recapped the pill bottle. We went back onto the deck and I saw Davey eyeing the water jug.

"Can I drink some of that?" he asked.

"Of course," I said. "It's for you."

We sat down with the pack between us. Davey picked up the water, admired it like a Christmas present, and unscrewed the cap. He turned it up and took a couple of long swallows.

"Good," he said, catching his breath.

"You can't live on Dr Pepper."

"I know," he said. "I ran out yesterday."

"You haven't had anything to drink since yesterday?"

"I licked the dew off some leaves this mornin'. And I was gonna boil some creek water to make it safe."

"Geez. Drink some more."

Davey drank half the water in the jug while he watched me open one of the cans of ravioli and set it before him.

"Eat that," I said. "And a banana. I don't have a fork or anything."

Davey set the water down and stood up. "I've got one inside. I've got just about everything I need."

Davey went inside the camp and reappeared with a rusty fork. He sat and shoveled ravioli into his mouth.

"I remember this fork," he said while he chewed. "I found one of my old toy cars in there, too. It's just like we left it."

"Maybe I should call your dad when I get home," I said.

Davey took another bite and shook his head. "I don't know his phone number," he said in a matter-of-fact way.

"What about your brother?"

Davey shook his head again.

"How about your mom?"

"She's dead."

"Oh . . . Well, I can't keep bringing you things like this. My parents are gonna get suspicious."

"You don't have to," he said. "Just come and visit me."

"But you drank almost all the water I brought, and you can't just lick leaves every morning."

Davey ate the last of the ravioli and set his fork in the can. "I know," he said. "I'm gonna boil water."

I shoved a banana toward him. "Eat that. Keep eating all you want."

He grabbed the banana and started peeling it.

"Do you have matches?" I asked.

He shook his head as he took big bites.

"How are you gonna make a fire?" I asked.

Davey shrugged. "I'll figure it out. Indians did."

"I'll bring you some matches."

"What about boards? Can you bring me some?" he asked.

"Uh, maybe. Dad has a few pieces lying around that he didn't use for his projects."

"I'll pay you for it."

"You don't have to pay me, but it's gonna take more than just some scrap wood to fix this place up. And it might take a while."

Davey grabbed the other banana and began peeling it. "Well, I've been havin' to look for food most of the time."

"Yeah, I guess so."

"Have you caught any fish?" he asked me.

"No," I said. "I was looking for a dead body."

"Really?"

"Yeah. A man that got lost out here. Dad says he's probably dead since they haven't found him."

"That must be why the boats kept coming by and the helicopters were in the air."

"Yeah," I said. "You see them?"

Davey nodded. "I hid my canoe."

"Why?"

Davey kept chewing and didn't answer.

"Well," I continued, "I thought maybe I could find the body. But this swamp is bigger than I expected."

"What are you gonna do when you find it?"

"I guess tell the police. Get on the news and stuff."

"Yeah, that would be cool," Davey said.

He finished his second banana and looked at the hot dogs.

"They're cold," I said, "but they'll fill you up."

"I was thinkin' they'd make good fish bait," he said.

"I can't leave you my fishing rod. Dad would ask me about it."

Davey shook his head and stood up. "Don't need it. I found some fishin' line and hooks in the camp. And I had an idea."

Davey disappeared into the camp and came back with a wad of tangled line, rusty hooks, and a cooking pot. I watched as he sat down and poured the rest of the water out of the jug into the pot. Then he began untangling the line.

"I'm gonna tie a hook and line to the handle of the milk jug and float it out into the deep part of the creek like a big cork. I heard of it before. I'll bet I can catch somethin'."

I watched Davey's fingers working at the hopeless tangle.

Then I studied his face and the way he squinted his eyes. It was obvious that he couldn't see well.

"Davey," I said.

He didn't look up. "What?"

I didn't really plan on saying it, but it just came out of my mouth. "Are you telling me the truth?"

6

DAVEY KEPT WORKING AT THE TANGLED FISHING
line and didn't answer my question.

"Did you run away from somewhere?" I asked him.

His fingers continued to move, but I could see he wasn't concentrating on the line anymore.

"I'm just curious," I said. "I won't tell anybody."

He still wouldn't look at me, and I sensed he was growing uncomfortable.

"I told you," he said. "I'm waitin' on my brother. And Daddy."

I knew he wasn't telling me everything, but I decided maybe it wasn't any of my business. There were things I didn't want him to know about me, too. I reached out and pulled the tangled line away from him. "You'll never get that undone. I'll just pull some off my fishing reel."

He nodded and let me stuff the wad into my pocket.

"It's probably rotten anyway," I said.

I got my fishing rod out of the *Bream Chaser* and returned. I broke off my lure. Then I stripped about twenty feet of line from the reel, bit it off, and handed it to him.

"That ought to be enough for the jug, and maybe you can rig a fishing pole."

"Thanks," he said.

Davey took one end of the line and tried to thread it through the eye of one of the rusty fishhooks. It was hopeless.

"I'll help," I said.

He handed it to me. I got the line through the eye, then remembered that I still didn't know how to tie a fishing knot. I recalled what Dad had told me about twisting it and sticking the end back through the hole—but then it was too confusing and I felt the pressure of Davey watching my fingers. I tied a quick square knot and gave it back to him.

"That'll work," I said.

Davey put a piece of hot dog on the hook, stood, and tossed the jug into the creek. A cool breeze came over the tops of the trees and rippled the water. I thought about how lonely I'd be if I were by myself out here in this abandoned camp. I grabbed my fishing rod and backpack and stood up as well.

"Do you have a flashlight?" I asked him.

"I did. But it got wet and now it won't work."

"What do you do when it's dark?"

"I sit out here."

"And do what?"

"Just sit here and listen. There's owls and raccoons and stuff."

"Do you get scared?"

"Sometimes. I don't like goin' inside the camp after dark. You can't see anything in there."

It sounded awful.

"But the sheets will make it better," Davey said. "Thanks."

"I'll bring you some more stuff," I said.

Davey smiled. "Like wood?"

"Forget the wood. You need more food and water. Then you need something so you can see at night."

Davey nodded.

"Okay. I'll bring more food and water and a flashlight . . . and maybe some lumber."

Davey smiled again.

I looked back at the camp. "What tools do you have?"

"I've got a hammer."

"That's all?"

Davey nodded.

"I can get a handsaw and a tape measure."

"I got three pieces of roofin' tin from an old camp up a ways. I got it stacked on the ground."

"Do you have nails for it?" I asked.

"I've been pullin' old nails out of boards and usin' those."

"I'll bring some new nails. What else?"

"All of that sounds good."

"What about some fishing tackle?"

"Okay."

"You can have that lure I broke off . . . Matches? You need matches."

"Okay."

"And soap. You need to have a way to get clean."

"Okay."

"Anything else?" I asked again. "There's probably a lot I'm not thinking of."

"No, that's good," he said.

"I'll be back as soon as I can. But I have church tomorrow, and then I'm supposed to go stay the night at my friend's house. It might be Monday."

"What's your friend's name?"

"Grover Middleton."

"Is he pretty cool?"

"Not at all," I said. And it felt good to finally say it out loud. "I don't even want to go over there, but he keeps bugging me."

Davey smiled the tiniest bit, like he thought something was funny.

"You gonna be okay?" I said.

"Yeah," he said. "I'll be okay. I'll see you Monday."

When I got back to our dock I fastened the *Bream Chaser* to the cleat and thought about how I could get one for Davey. Then I started up to the house and came across Dad in the yard working on the sprinkler system. He was still in his gym clothes from working out at the precinct fitness center.

"Any fish?" he asked.

I shook my head.

"Well, don't get discouraged."

"I just rode around mostly. Exploring, you know."

"Did you stop off and show Grover your new boat?"

"Not yet," I said. "I'm spending the night at his house tomorrow. I'll show it to him then."

Fortunately, Dad didn't ask any more questions. He knelt in the grass and inspected the sprinkler head he'd dug up.

"Hey, Dad?"

He got some pliers out of his pocket and began twisting at the water pipe. "Yeah, son?"

"Isn't it illegal to have camps in the swamp?"

"You mean east of the Pascagoula River?"

"Right."

"It's mostly conservation land now."

"So you can't just go out there and build something?"

He looked back at me, his hands still working. "I don't think so. Why do you ask?"

Suddenly I was sorry I'd brought it up.

"I was just wondering," I said.

Dad grabbed a screwdriver lying near his foot and started tightening a screw inside the sprinkler head.

"I know a guy with the marine police who patrols the

area," Dad continued. "He tells me people get into all kinds of trouble out there."

I swallowed nervously and turned to go.

"Best to stay out of it," he said. "We've got all the water we need close to home."

So there it was. He'd basically told me the swamp was off-limits. But I'd told Davey I would bring him supplies. And he didn't have enough to live on anywhere, much less in an abandoned swamp camp. My brain went to work, twisting Dad's words into what I wanted them to be. He hadn't said *not* to go out there. He'd just said it was *best* not to go out there.

"I'm headed inside," I said.

I started for the back door. It felt like a rope was tugging my conscience in two directions at once. Neither one of them good.

7

SUNDAY MORNING DAD APPEARED DRESSED IN HIS
Sunday suit. He told me he had to go to the station for a
couple of hours before he met us at church. There had been a
shootout with some gang members and two of his officers
that night, and he needed to make a statement to the press.

I rode to First Methodist with Mom. She has a Nissan
Altima that isn't nearly as cool a car as Dad's, but it's tidy
and smart like she is.

"Do you ever worry about Dad getting shot?" I asked.

She pulled up to a four-way stop, flipped down the visor
mirror, and checked her makeup.

"Of course I do," she said. "But I believe in what he does,
and I knew what I was getting into when I married him. You
know, I thought about attending the police academy at one
time."

"Seriously? You?"

Mom smiled. "Sam, your mother's not all paintings. She
knows how to take care of herself."

"I just can't see it."

"Well, in the end, I didn't either. Both your dad and I would have had long hours and crazy schedules, and it's hard to raise a family like that."

"I guess so," I said. "But that would have been cool."

Mom reached over and playfully poked me in the leg. "I've outgrown cool."

Dad arrived just before service started and squeezed into the pew with us. When the preacher came out and began his sermon, it wasn't long before Dad was drumming his fingers on his thigh. I knew his knee would start jumping next and he'd get up and go to the restroom at least once to walk some of it off. Sometimes Mom could calm him by reaching across me and tapping his shoulder, but it just wasn't easy for him to sit still for long.

In spite of Dad's restlessness in church, he rarely missed service. He knew attending as a family meant a lot to Mom, and it was obvious he just did it for her—and did the best he could with it. Dad was all about people doing their duty and tending to their responsibilities, and church was one of his.

For me, church was thinking time. I thought about Davey. I imagined the two of us repairing the old camp together and making a sort of clubhouse out of it. A place where I could come visit him and even spend the night sometime. A place where I'd be important, where I'd be the one who was cool and knew about things. Things I could do that no else could. Then, like most fantasies, the perfect picture I'd built in my mind was slowly taken down by reality. Davey's dad and brother would be there soon, and I'd be an outsider again.

After service the congregation gathered in the fellowship hall for doughnuts, milk, and coffee. It wasn't long before I saw a red tuft of hair bobbing toward me through the crowd. In a moment Grover's big pasty-white face was staring at me like I had some explaining to do.

"What?" I said. "I told you I'm coming over."

"When?"

"This afternoon. In my boat."

"When did you get a boat?"

"I told you yesterday I was out in my boat."

"No, you said you were out in *the* boat."

Grover's always precise and remembers everything.

"Well, whatever," I said. "I got it on my birthday. It's called the *Bream Chaser*. I got some fishing stuff, too."

"Why?"

"Because I told Dad I wanted to learn to fish."

"Why?"

"I just told you why."

Grover stared at me a moment. "Well," he finally said, "I found a portal. When you get to my house I'll show you level six."

"Fine," I said. "See you in a little while."

Grover turned abruptly and walked away, satisfied that his mission was complete. I watched him go and wondered how I'd ever found anything to like about him. Then I saw Natalia, their housekeeper, waiting for him at the door. She's Argentinean, about Mom's age, and I'd always thought she was pretty. But I'd never seen her at our church before, and Mrs. Middleton was nowhere to be seen. I thought that was strange.

Mom left ahead of us in her car while I climbed into Dad's Tahoe. It's all white, with the City of Pascagoula Police Department emblem on the doors, a brush guard with a winch on the front, strobe lights on top, and a spotlight on the driver side. It was probably the coolest truck I'd ever seen, and people stared at us everywhere we went. I pulled the heavy door shut and sank into the big leather seat.

Dad let out a sigh of relief. "All right," he said.

"Doughnuts were good," I commented, just to say something.

He looked into the side mirror and began to pull out into traffic. Dad's a cool driver. It's not just the dark sunglasses and the Tahoe; it's also in the way he works the steering wheel with only the palm of his left hand. His other hand remains on the seat near his waist, where he usually has his pistol holstered. Like he could draw and shoot without even slowing down.

Dad pulled onto the highway and accelerated, and it felt like he was in charge of everything again, even the truck engine itself. I sat back and faced forward and thought about Davey and the swamp.

"Have you ever hit a log out there?" I asked him.

Dad must have been thinking about something else, and it took him a moment to respond.

"You mean in the boat? On the river?"

"Yes, sir."

"Once or twice. It happens . . . which reminds me that I need to show you about the shear pin."

"What's that?"

Whatever he'd been thinking about had crept into his head again.

"I'll show you when we get home," he said.

He came up fast behind the car ahead. It seemed like he was always in a hurry, always distracted. I imagined work stuff and home projects and ideas fluttering in his head like leaves in a tornado. He palmed the steering wheel to the left, gassed the engine, and roared around the car like it was sitting still. Whenever I was alone with him I wondered what he thought about me, if he thought about me much at all. I felt like something he just hauled around with him and tried to like. Like something he just had to attend to out of a sense of duty. Like church.

Dad stopped at a gas station to fill up. I stayed in the car as he got out, slid his credit card, and began fueling the Tahoe. Only a few seconds had gone by before I heard some commotion to my right. I looked over just in time to see a big man in flip-flops running across the parking lot. A woman appeared at the door of the convenience store, yelling something at him that I couldn't understand. Then suddenly I heard the pump nozzle clatter to the ground. Dad jumped into the Tahoe and started the engine. He reached over and pressed me back against the seat with his hand.

"Hold on," he said.

He punched the accelerator and the tires squealed on the pavement. I saw the man in the distance, running across an overgrown field. Dad took his hand off me and reached for his radio.

"Three-One requesting backup. Pursuit in progress at 7204 Martin Bluff Road."

"Copy that, Thirty-One," the station dispatcher replied. "Backup en route."

Dad dropped the radio on the seat again and grabbed the steering wheel with both hands. We slammed into a small ditch, then bounced out of it and tore across the grassy field in pursuit of the runner. Everything was happening so fast that I didn't have time to be afraid. I just gripped the armrest tightly and stared ahead.

"Dispatch to Thirty-One," the radio said.

Dad didn't answer. He had all of his attention focused on the runner. When we were about ten yards behind the man, Dad spun the steering wheel and the Tahoe fishtailed, kicking up grass and mud and coming within a few feet of mowing the man down. The runner kept going as we came to a stop, and Dad threw the Tahoe into park.

"Stay here!" he shouted to me.

Dad leaped out and gave chase. I realized since he was in plainclothes he didn't have his pistol on him. He tackled the man, and I watched them both fall and disappear into the tall field grass.

"Dispatch to Thirty-One," I heard again.

I looked at the radio on Dad's seat, then back up at the grass. I saw the big man sitting up and punching down. Then he was out of sight again, and I saw Dad start to stand. Suddenly he was falling, and then he was gone and the big man was punching again. I knew something was going wrong. I grabbed the radio.

"This is Sam Ford!" I yelled into the receiver. "My dad's in trouble!"

"Please identify yourself," the dispatcher said calmly.

"Sam Ford! Thirty-One!"

I dropped the radio onto the floor and leaped out of the cruiser and started running toward them.

"Stop!" I yelled.

8

BEFORE I REACHED THE STRUGGLE DAD APPEARED out of the grass with the suspect, whose arm he'd wrenched behind his back. They were both breathing hard, their faces red and grass hanging from their hair. Then two police cruisers came skidding up next to me and three officers leaped out. They took the suspect from Dad and dragged him away.

Dad watched them for a moment, then walked over to me and grabbed my arm and pulled me back to the Tahoe. Once we were at the car again he let go and turned and leaned against the hood. He was still breathing hard. He swiped his face with the back of his hand and looked at a streak of blood on it.

"Christ," he said.

"Dad?" I said.

He looked over at me. He took a deep breath through his nose. "I told you to stay put," he said.

I looked at my feet.

"Get back in the car," he said firmly. "And stay there."

I watched from the passenger seat while Dad stood outside

and cleaned his face with a hand towel that one of the other policemen brought him. They talked for a while; then the policeman turned to go, and Dad came and got back in the Tahoe. He wiped his face once more and dropped the bloody towel onto the floor.

"Do you need to go to the hospital, Dad?" I asked.

He started the car.

"Dad?"

He looked over at me. "What the hell were you thinking, Sam?"

"I didn't know what to do. I thought he was going to . . ."

Dad shook his head and looked away and put the Tahoe in drive. The other policemen were gone now, and we pulled out of the field and onto the highway.

I couldn't take my eyes off his messed-up face. "You're still bleeding," I said.

"I'll be okay," he said.

"You didn't have your gun. I thought he was going to kill you."

Dad wiped his cheek with his shirtsleeve and looked over at me. "Exactly how did you think you were gonna help that situation?"

"I don't know."

"I don't know either," he finally said.

He didn't say anything to me the rest of the way home. I stared out the window feeling small and confused.

• • •

When we stepped through the front door of our house, Mom took one look at Dad and walked away toward the bathroom without a word. He leaned against the kitchen counter, and she reappeared with alcohol and bandages and cotton swabs.

"Got into a scuffle at the gas station," he told her.

"I see," she said.

"Some guy tried to rob it. Acted like he had a gun."

She put some alcohol on a swab and started dabbing at his face.

"He almost got the best of me before my backup got there." Dad glanced at me.

"Stay still," Mom said.

"Sam decided he was gonna try and help out."

Mom stopped and looked me over. "What?"

"I told him to stay in the car," Dad said.

"Dad didn't have his gun," I said. "I thought the man was gonna kill him."

"Are you hurt?"

"No, ma'am," I said. "It was just for a few seconds. Then the other policemen got there."

Mom grabbed a small bandage off the counter and tore it open. I could see she was getting angry. "Seriously, Roger," she said. "Did you have to get involved in that? On your day off."

"What was I supposed to do, Margie?"

"When our son's in the car?"

Dad turned to her. "I wouldn't have—"

Mom forced his chin away from her. "Stay still," she said again.

"I had it under control," he said.

"It doesn't sound like it."

"I'm okay, Mom," I said.

She turned to me. Mom doesn't get angry often, but when she does, she's got a hard look that bores right through a person. "Sam, I'm not happy with you either. When your father tells you to do something, you do it. Understand?"

I looked down and nodded. Mom looked at Dad again and pressed the bandage to his cheek.

"Go and get cleaned up for lunch, Sam," she muttered.

I walked back to my room feeling even worse.

No one said anything at the table. I felt the weight of Mom's anger hanging over me, and it was hard to eat. Even Dad seems to get uneasy when Mom's not happy. He picked at his food and shifted in his chair and sighed a couple of times. I was relieved when he finally stood and broke the silence.

"Come on, Sam," he said. "I'll show you about the shear pin."

He showed me where the extra pin was kept in a small plastic bag under the engine cowling. It was a metal pin about half the size of a matchstick. Then he got into the *Bream Chaser*, pulled out his Leatherman multitool, and showed me how to remove the cotter key on the prop and slide it off. He pointed to the drive shaft, where I saw another one of those pins sitting crossways in it.

"It's designed to break if you hit something," he said. "So the prop will free-spin instead of losing a blade. You just slip a new pin in there, and you're good. You can even use a nail or a stick in an emergency."

Learning about the shear pin only made me wonder just how many more things there were that he hadn't thought to show me.

"But you shouldn't have to worry too much about hitting things in the bayou," he said. "Just stick to the middle of the waterway and you'll be fine."

I looked up at him and nodded that I understood, but mostly I was looking at the bruises starting on his cheeks and the trace of dried blood around the rim of his nostril.

I can never be as good as him, I thought. *And he knows it.*

9

I DROVE THE *BREAM CHASER* TO GROVER'S THAT
afternoon and tied it to his dock. His and his dad's boats hung
in the lifts, freshly waxed, all the ropes coiled precisely and the
engines covered with canvas slips like they'd just been deliv-
ered. The lawn sloped down the creek bank, as neatly cut as a
golf course. Leading up to their multilevel house was a stone
walk, edged with monkey grass. The place was like a country
club ready for a party that never seemed to happen.

Dr. Middleton worked even more than Dad, and Mrs.
Middleton traveled a lot. In addition to cleaning the house,
Natalia cooked and drove Grover to school. It felt to me like
he was a prince in his own mansion. Except he didn't seem to
notice all the expensive things around him. All he did was
stay holed up in the basement. I imagined if that one cinder-
block room were transported to the middle of a desert, as
long as the electricity worked and he didn't have to go outside, he'd be fine.

I shouldered my backpack and walked up the lawn. The
French doors leading into the lower level of their house were

always unlocked. I slipped inside and crossed through a sitting room I'd never seen them use and then through another door into the basement that I thought of as Grover's lair.

"Still at level six," he mumbled without looking up.

I thought about telling Grover of Dad's scuffle that morning, but then I figured he wouldn't understand or even care. I crossed the room to a bunk bed and threw my backpack onto the top bunk. Grover's official bedroom was upstairs, but he never slept in it. He showered, dressed, ate, and slept in the lair. It seemed he only used his real room as storage for clean clothes. His dirty clothes were usually strewn across the basement floor until Natalia picked them up, washed them, and took them upstairs again. Along one wall of the lair were his refrigerator and a counter with a sink and a microwave. There were also a pool table and a foosball table that I'd never seen him use. Littered across the tops of them were soda cans and empty cartons of instant macaroni and cheese and crumpled bags of microwave popcorn. Blankets were tossed on the floor in front of the television and over the sofa like he'd been nesting in them.

I dug through one of the blankets until I found the extra game controller. Then I brushed some popcorn kernels off the sofa cushions and plopped down next to him. I stared at the television and tried to get my head back into Demon Quest.

"All right," I said. "What do I do?"

It didn't take long before Grover caught me up to where he was in the game and I was sucked into his furious world of monster fighting.

After three mind-numbing hours, we'd destroyed the demon at level six and our muscled warriors stood on the precipice of a high cliff, staring over a fresh battleground swarming with new breeds of nightmarish beasts and presenting a challenge that seemed more impossible than ever.

Grover dropped his controller to the floor. "Done," he said, like it had been easy. Another life milestone for him. "Next up, level seven."

I set my controller beside me, mentally exhausted.

Grover got up and crossed to his refrigerator and pulled out a Coke. He popped it open and took two big gulps like he needed it.

"We going to eat supper?" I said.

"Get anything you want," he said. "There's some Hot Pockets in the freezer."

"Is anybody else here?"

Grover took another long swallow. "I think Natalia's around," he said. "Dad'll probably be home later."

I got up and went to his refrigerator and opened the freezer. It was stacked full of pepperoni Hot Pockets.

"Don't you ever get sick of these things?"

"You don't like them?"

"Well, I do. It's just a lot of them."

"Just fuel, man," he said.

Hearing Grover say "man" like he was anything close to cool was annoying. But I didn't respond; I just grabbed one of the frozen packages, unwrapped it, and stuck it in the microwave. I pressed *start*, then watched the food turn slowly on the platter. I felt Grover studying me like my parents.

"There might be something else in the refrigerator upstairs," he said.

I didn't want to look at him. I imagined a bowl on the floor and Natalia coming downstairs throughout the day and refilling it with dog food for Grover. His fuel.

"I'm already cooking this," I said. "It's fine."

After a minute he said, "So you came in your boat?"

"Yeah," I said. "I came in my boat. What'd you think?"

"So what's the big deal about it?"

I felt myself getting shoved into a mental corner where I didn't want to be.

"I don't know," I said. "I like it. What's wrong with that?"

"You don't call me anymore. That's what's wrong."

That annoying Annie hair, I thought. *That annoying face.*

I looked at him. "Geez, Grover. I'm over here *now*, aren't I? You expect everybody to sit in your basement with you and play video games their whole life?"

"It's not your whole life," he said flatly.

I studied the digital timer on the microwave and didn't answer.

"You haven't even shown me your boat," he said.

I turned to him again. I couldn't hold back any longer. "Seriously?" I asked. "It's right out there tied to your dock! You know that! If you really cared, you would've asked me about it earlier, but we had to sit here for three hours and get to stupid level seven!"

Grover looked perplexed. "I told you that's what we were going to do," he said.

"It's always about what *you* want! Maybe I *hate* Demon Quest!"

"No you don't," he said.

The microwave began beeping, but I didn't make a move toward it. I was shaking, and I was both mad and nervous. I'd never acted like that toward anyone.

"Why are you yelling at me?" he said.

I started breathing heavily through my nose, trying to calm down.

"Your Hot Pocket's ready," he said.

"I don't care about the stupid Hot Pocket," I muttered.

"What's wrong with you?" he said.

I shook my head. "You're so clueless."

"About what?"

"About everything!"

He stared at me.

I took another deep breath. "You don't even think about it, do you?"

"About what?"

"Leroy. Gooch. The fight."

He didn't answer.

"In case I need to remind you, you got beat up in front of the entire school, Grover."

His face twitched the slightest bit. "So did you," he said.

"Yeah, I did."

"So?"

Words came out of me like they'd forced their way through a door I'd been holding shut. "So maybe if I wasn't hanging out with you, it wouldn't have happened to me."

Grover started to reply, then stopped himself. Then he said, "What does that mean?"

"It means I'm tired of being a loser! I don't want to be in this basement in this empty house playing video games and eating Hot Pockets!"

He kept watching me until I had to turn away. I happened to look at the microwave. I stared at it for a moment, words buzzing in my head like hornets. Finally I punched the button for the door and pulled out the Hot Pocket and tossed it on the counter.

"We don't have to play anymore," he said.

I struggled to calm the noise in my head. "I just want to go home," I mumbled.

"Okay," he said in an empty way. It was like his brain had finally come up against something it couldn't understand.

"But it's dark," I said. "I can't take out the boat in the dark."

"What do you want to do? We'll do what you want to do."

"I want to go to bed."

Grover picked my Hot Pocket off the counter.

"You eat it," I said. "I'm not hungry."

I climbed onto Grover's top bunk and lay there staring at the ceiling while he walked about the room and shut off the lights. Then I listened to him climb into bed below me. I felt sick over what I'd said to him, but I didn't know how to fix any of it. I'd told him the truth about how I felt, and there was nothing I could think to say that would erase it.

We both lay there in the dark room, neither of us talking. After a while I heard Grover get out of bed again. "I'm going to my room," he said.

I didn't respond. I watched him walk to the staircase and heard him going up the stairs. Then I was alone in his lair, and I never thought the place could feel so sad. I wasn't ready to feel as bad as I did. I'd never felt so lonely. I considered going after him and telling him I was sorry and suggesting that we stay up and play video games all night and act like nothing happened. Then I thought that if I did, I wouldn't be solving anything. I'd still feel the same way about him. I just had to get through the night. I had to be like Davey, out there alone in the swamp like he wasn't even a real boy but something in my imagination. I wished more than anything that I was out there with him. And I thought maybe Davey and his camp were the most real thing in my life.

10

THE NEXT MORNING I WOKE EARLY, GATHERED MY
backpack, and slipped out of the Middletons' basement. When
I drove away from their dock I had the sense that I'd never
see or hear from Grover again. It was a sick, reckless feeling
that didn't sit right with me at all. But I tried to put it behind
me and concentrate on what lay ahead.

Davey.

Flashlight
Matches
Books
Jug of water
Canned food
Milk for Baldy

He doesn't know anything about me.

Fishhooks
Fishing line

Handsaw
Nails
Scrap lumber

I can be whatever I want around him.

When I got home Dad had already left for work. Mom fixed breakfast for me. She watched me eating for a moment, and I could tell she wanted to say something.

"Sam," she said, "I just want you to make good decisions. That's all I ask."

"I know," I said.

"That's all. That's one thing I was upset about yesterday. But I was also upset with your father for putting you in that situation to begin with."

"I know," I said.

Mom left to get her things together and go to work at the church for a couple of hours. After she was gone I sat at my desk and thought about the decision I had already made. I knew Mom wouldn't approve, but it seemed an even worse decision to abandon Davey after I'd promised to help him.

So I picked up my pen and made a list of the items I'd thought of to take him. Then I went around the house collecting them and adding a few more as they got my attention.

Salt
Pepper
Kitchen knife

Plastic lawn bags
Pillow

I poured the salt and pepper into two sandwich bags so that the shakers wouldn't be missed. The pillow was an old one from the storage room. I doubted anyone would even remember it. I stuffed everything into one of the plastic lawn bags and took it out to the *Bream Chaser*. Then I took the wheelbarrow from the garage and collected some of Dad's scrap lumber and the handsaw and some nails from the storage shed. Dad probably didn't need the lumber and rarely used the handsaw, but he knew where everything was and noticed anything out of place. I was going to have to think hard to come up with an explanation for what I was taking.

I wheeled the lumber and tools out to the boat and organized it all on the floor and seats so that the weight was evenly distributed. Finally, I left Mom a note in the kitchen saying that I was going fishing and wouldn't be back until later that afternoon.

As I raced past Grover's house again I didn't turn to look but held it in the corner of my eye like it was just another home along the way with people living in it I didn't know. And when I headed out onto the river, the blue skies and shimmering water and freedom lay before me like an easy escape from it all.

I breathed easy, felt the cool wind in my face, and smoothly navigated the turns like I'd been running the same route for years. Despite all the things the counselor and my parents had told me, this was the answer. This was what made me feel like myself again. It had been so easy all along. I couldn't imagine not having figured it out—having spent too many weeks boxed up with Grover in my misery.

Davey was waiting for me on the deck when I arrived at the swamp camp. I tied up and got out with my bag of supplies and walked past him. He followed without a word, like he'd known what to expect of me all along and I'd known the same of him.

He watched as I emptied the lawn bag onto the floor of the camp.

"I've got some boards in the boat, too," I said. "It should be enough to get you going. You can collect wood to put in that old charcoal grill and use the matches I brought to light it so you can cook fish."

"You brought a jug, too," he said.

"Yeah, you can pour the water into your pot and use the jug for another fishing rig."

"I caught some," he said. "You wanna see?"

"You did? Sure."

Davey led me outside to the end of the dock, where he pulled up a stringer with five tremendous catfish on it.

"Wow!" I said. "Those things are huge!"

Davey smiled proudly. "Yeah," he said. "You wanna eat one?"

"Now?"

"Yeah, I'm pretty hungry. I tried rubbin' some sticks together to start a fire, but I couldn't make it work."

"Okay," I said. "I'll try to get the grill going if you know how to clean the fish."

"I know how," he said. "Daddy taught me. He used to take me fishing on the bridge."

"Good," I said. "I've never cleaned a fish myself."

"You just get the guts out and scrape off the scales."

"Fine," I said. "You can use the knife I brought you."

Davey took one of the catfish off the stringer and used the kitchen knife to gut it. Meanwhile I found some old newspaper and scrap wood and started a fire in the grill.

"How's Baldy?" I asked.

"He's good. I got him to drink some more."

"I brought another thing of milk," I said.

"I saw it. Thanks."

After a few minutes Davey brought the gutted fish to me. It wasn't long before we stood over it as it sizzled on the grate. It didn't look like anything from the grocery store, but Davey couldn't take his eyes off it.

"Gonna be good," he said.

I sprinkled some salt and pepper over it. "Better than canned food," I said.

He looked at me with that excitement in his eyes. "Got everything I need now," he said.

I frowned. "I don't know about that. But you've got enough to live on for a while."

We tested the fish meat with Davey's fork until we found it flaky and falling off the bones. Then we put it on the deck and sat around it and picked at it with our fingers. It wasn't nearly as good as Mom's, but Davey ate it like it was the best thing he'd ever tasted. When we were done there wasn't anything left but the skeleton and the head.

"Keep the grill going and you can cook more later," I said.

We spent a few hours sawing the lumber into sizes Davey needed for planks. Then we used a few of the scrap two-by-fours to repair the rotten rafters so that he could replace the tin on the roof. It was sweaty work. Heat shimmered off the underside of the tin, the thrumming of cicadas filled the air, and dirt daubers floated in and out of the camp. But I couldn't remember enjoying work so much.

As the sun sank below the treetops we sat on the end of the deck, hanging our feet over the marsh grass and passing the water jug between us.

"When you gotta go?" he asked me.

I didn't want to think about it.

"Pretty soon," I said. "I can't be out after dark."

"Why?"

"My parents won't allow it."

"You have both a mom and a dad?"

"Well, yeah. What did you think?"

Davey didn't answer my question. "You wanna take a fish back with you?" he asked.

It suddenly struck me as a good idea. I was going to have to bring a fish home at some point or Dad would get suspicious.

"Sure," I said.

"You can show it to your parents."

"That's what I was thinking."

"Then maybe they'll let you come back and see me," he said.

"Your dad and brother might be here soon."

"You can still come see us," he said. "All of us."

I hesitated. "Maybe so," I said.

"How about tomorrow?"

"I don't know," I said.

Davey looked down and I saw disappointment flow over him.

"I'll try," I said. "I really want to."

He nodded to himself as I grabbed my backpack and stood.

"I better go," I said.

Davey got another fish from the stringer and gave it to me before I shoved off. "Your dad'll like that one," he said.

I took the fish and put it into the bait well after filling

it with fresh water. Then I went to the stern and started the engine. As I motored away from the camp I wasn't sure how I was going to pull off more trips into the swamp, but I knew I wanted to come back and visit Davey more than anything. And I knew that somehow I'd find a way.

11

WHEN I ARRIVED AT OUR DOCK IT WAS ALMOST
dark. Dad came out of the house to help me get the *Bream
Chaser* into the lift. By the time he reached me I already had
the front and back hooks attached.

"We were getting a little worried about you, son," he said.
But I could tell by the way he said it that he was proud I
seemed to have been out enjoying myself.

"I guess I lost track of time," I said.

Dad flipped the switch to start the hoist, and I put on my
backpack and handed him my fishing rod. Then I reached
into the bait well and pulled out the catfish.

"Well, well," he said. "What do we have here?"

"Catfish," I said.

"I see that. Congratulations. I told you it just takes a little
patience. Did it pull hard?"

"Not really."

"Well, it's sure a nice one. Go on and take it inside, and
we'll clean it in the kitchen. I'll handle the boat."

"Okay," I said.

I started up the dock toward the house, feeling hollow. I told myself that next time I was going to catch my own fish and put the lies behind me.

Mom cooked the fish for dinner that night, but I wasn't hungry for it. I picked at the meat and ate a little bit and spread the rest around. I didn't feel as guilty about Grover or the lies as I did about leaving Davey. I pictured him out there alone in the big swamp, sawing and hammering and cooking fish. And at night, sitting on the rotten deck and staring at the still water of the creek.

His brother and his dad will get there soon, I thought to myself. But for some reason I couldn't imagine Davey as anything but alone.

It was unusually dark in my room when I woke Tuesday morning. I looked out the window and saw the sky covered with a thick blanket of gray clouds. The bayou was calm and still, with breezy patches of ripple blowing across it. I got up and went into the living room and found Mom watching the news.

"Looks like a tropical storm's headed this way," she said.

"How bad is it?" I asked.

"Just a little stretch of nasty weather."

I immediately thought about Davey. "Like a hurricane?"

"Nothing like that, but it's going to be very rainy and windy. Your father's coming home in a couple of hours and wants your help getting things ready."

"Yes, ma'am," I said.

By late morning it was sprinkling rain. I heard Dad pull into the driveway and watched through the window as he got out of the car wearing his police rain gear. He hurried around the side of the house to the dock, and I put on my parka and went out the back door to help. The *Bream Chaser* was fine in the lift once we raised it as high as it could go. Next we hauled the dock chairs up to the yard and around the side of the house, where they wouldn't blow away. Then we stowed away the grill and some other porch furniture, plus a few small planters.

The rain increased steadily for the rest of the day. I stayed inside on the living room sofa and watched television. I purposely avoided the Xbox because I would have felt guilty playing it after what I'd said to Grover. And then I thought about him alone in his lair and wondered if he even cared about what I had said to him.

Mostly I thought about Davey. I wished there was some means to check on him or at least get him a message. But there was no way to sneak out with Mom at home and the weather like it was. So I sat there feeling helpless, hoping the storm wouldn't last long.

● ● ●

Wednesday morning the wind was tossing the treetops and gusting around the sides of the house. Now the rain came in cold slanted sheets, pelting the windowpanes. Dad had to go back to the station because everyone on the force was on call until the storm was over. Mom and I were left alone again, listening to the weather beat on the windows. I couldn't stop worrying about Davey sitting in the camp with water dripping around him. I didn't remember him having a raincoat. I didn't remember him having any clothes other than the torn ones he was wearing. I wished I'd paid attention to the weather report and brought him some gear.

It stormed the rest of the day. I helped Mom make a salad and a big lasagna casserole for dinner, which she kept warming in the oven for when Dad got home. That evening I was lying on the living room sofa trying not to think about my growling stomach when I heard the front door open. I sat up and turned to see Dad on the stoop taking off his rain slicker. Behind him was a man I didn't know. After they were both done shaking off their coats and hanging them on the railing they came inside. The stranger wore a uniform, but it wasn't one I recognized. He was slightly shorter than Dad but solidly built. He had a pistol holstered on his side and wore a tight, serious expression.

Mom, hearing the commotion, came in off the sun porch. "Hello," she said.

"Good evening," the man said.

Dad waved me over. "Son, come here and meet Officer Stockton."

I got up and walked around the sofa and approached the man.

"Jim, this is my wife, Margie, and my son, Sam."

"Nice to meet you all," he said.

Officer Stockton held out his hand to shake. I took it, and his grip was as solid as his stare. My eyes traveled across his shirt to the emblem on his breast pocket: PASCAGOULA MARINE POLICE.

My heart felt like it skipped a beat.

"Sam and I kept ourselves busy this afternoon making lasagna," Mom said. "Won't you stay for supper?"

"Thank you, Margie," Officer Stockton replied. "If it's no trouble."

"None at all," Mom said, and walked toward the kitchen.

I started following her to help when Dad called me back.

"Sam," Dad said, "I told Officer Stockton about your new boat. He wants to talk to you about something."

12

WE SAT DOWN IN THE LIVING ROOM. I WAS ON THE sofa next to Dad, and Officer Stockton took a wingback chair across from us. The rain continued to pelt the windows, and the room seemed suddenly small and cagelike.

"Officer Stockton knows just about all there is to know about the Pascagoula River system, son. I told him you've been out fishing the bayou and exploring."

"I mostly patrol south of here," Officer Stockton said.

He had a stern, flat way of speaking that made me uneasy.

"Most of the boat traffic's around the mouth of the river and out in the Gulf," he continued. "But we've had some strange things going on in the past few weeks. I was wondering if you'd seen anything unusual?"

"Like what?" I said.

"We found an abandoned boat out there. You probably saw that on the news. And I'm sure you saw the search and rescue teams looking for whoever was in it."

"Yes, sir," I said.

Officer Stockton glanced at Dad. "The vessel wasn't registered, and we couldn't track down the hull ID on it. I don't know if we'll ever get to the bottom of that one."

"I haven't seen any dead bodies," I said.

Officer Stockton paused a moment. Then he said, "No, I imagine we'd have heard about it if you did. Besides, we're talking about a search grid a good bit north of here. Up in the management area. I'm sure you don't get up that far, do you?"

I swallowed and shook my head. Out of the corner of my eye I saw Dad watching me. One more lie.

"I didn't think so," Officer Stockton continued. "But there's something else we're looking into that hits a little closer to home."

He waited like I was supposed to respond.

"You know the fish market just south of Kings Bayou?" he continued.

"Yes, sir. I mean, I haven't been there in my boat, but I know about it."

"Place got robbed about two weeks ago. Somebody saw an aluminum jon boat, sixteen or eighteen feet long, speed off about two o'clock in the morning."

"I'm not ever out that late," I said.

"I don't expect you are, but that boat's likely to be around here somewhere. It headed north, and I can tell you there's nowhere to go north of here, nowhere to take out. It's somebody who knows this river. It's just a swamp for miles up that way, and a fellow can get lost and hurt real easy."

"I haven't seen anything like that," I said.

"Well, like I told your dad, I can't get up here all that often, and it's good to have an extra set of eyes on things."

"Yes, sir," I said.

"Just anything unusual. Any strange boats or people. Anything."

I nodded.

Dad turned to me. "What do you think about that, son? You want to help out Officer Stockton?"

"I guess," I said.

"Dinner's on the table," Mom called.

I stood quickly and started for the dining room.

The lasagna was served with garlic bread and a Caesar salad. Officer Stockton sat stiffly in his chair and told Mom and me how good it all looked. Then we said grace and began eating. After a moment Mom asked Officer Stockton how he'd come to be in law enforcement.

He wiped the corner of his mouth with his napkin and replaced it in his lap. Then he began to tell us about himself in a factual way, like he was reciting an official report he wrote for dinner parties.

He'd grown up in Biloxi. After high school he joined the army and served two tours in Iraq. He received an honorable discharge in his late twenties, came home, enrolled at the police academy, and became a marine policeman. He'd been a law enforcement officer in Pascagoula ever since, except for two years when he'd lived in Houston, Texas.

"What took you to Houston?" Dad asked.

"My son had a brain tumor," he replied. "We moved there so he could get treatment."

"I'm sorry to hear that. I hope he's doing okay."

"He died two years ago."

Dad reached for his glass of water and nodded considerately.

"That must have been hard," Mom said.

"It's not something I wish on anyone," Officer Stockton replied.

Dad sipped his water and set it down. Officer Stockton picked up his fork and looked down at his plate and cut another precise bite of lasagna.

Mom broke the silence. "Where is your wife from?" she asked.

"Janet's from Biloxi," he said. "We grew up together."

"I've known Roger since middle school," Mom said. "I suppose some of us find each other early. Roger, why don't you tell Jim how we met?"

Dad appeared relieved to have something to say. He set his fork down and began telling the story I'd heard before. He'd missed the football team's bus and had to ride to the game in the bus with the cheerleaders. He'd never been so embarrassed and humiliated in his life, but he decided to make the best of it and sit next to Mom, who he thought was the prettiest girl in school. When they got to the game the rest of the team was waiting in the parking lot to tease him. He said he smiled and didn't hear a word they said.

Officer Stockton chuckled. "Sounds like a good way to travel," he said.

"Roger has a way of accidentally being at the right place at the right time," Mom added with a half smile. I couldn't help but think she was referencing the incident Dad had had at the gas station.

"Hey," Dad said jokingly, "I try."

Mom rolled her eyes at Dad and smirked. "But he always seems to come out of it okay," she said. "Somehow."

Apparently Mom wasn't upset with Dad anymore.

I thought about being trapped on a school bus with Julia. And sitting next to her. Then I imagined the other kids murmuring and pointing at me and her scooting away from me like I had a disease.

Dad told Officer Stockton about moving down from McComb when he got the job as chief of police and renting a cottage in town until we got our house built on the bayou. Finally they began to discuss the new liquefied natural gas facility being built at the mouth of the river. Dad felt it was a likely target for terrorism, and he had some ideas on how their two organizations could work together to keep it secure.

I hurried through the rest of my supper, then leaned over and told Mom I was tired.

"Go on," she said. "I think these two might be a while."

I stood to go, and Officer Stockton stopped talking and I felt him watching me.

"Nice meeting you, Sam," he said.

"You too," I said.

"Be safe out there in your boat," he said. "And keep your eyes open."

"Yes, sir," I said. "I will."

I lay in my bed that night listening to the rain, unable to sleep. I imagined the wind tearing the roof from the swamp camp and Davey clinging to the bunk bed, fearing for his life. Until I had to get it out of my head, and I couldn't think of anything to distract me but turning on the Xbox and playing Demon Quest until I fell asleep. Then I thought about Grover and told myself that I wasn't going to feel guilty just because of him. That I needed to do it just to spite him.

I got up and flipped on the television and the Xbox and grabbed the controller. I fully expected Grover to see me come online. His Xbox was never turned off. He was always online, even when he wasn't playing. And I made up my mind that I was going to have to ignore him if he started texting me. I signed on, but to my disbelief and relief, Grover wasn't logged in.

13

THE NEXT MORNING IT WAS STILL RAINING. I KEPT reminding myself that the swamp camp had been through storms as bad as Hurricane Katrina, that Davey might get wet but wasn't in any immediate danger. But I couldn't imagine him being anything but miserable.

Even if he wants to leave, he can't, I thought. *Not now. If he tries in that canoe, he'll die.*

More than once it crossed my mind to tell Dad about him and get Officer Stockton to go and help him. But I'd told Davey I wouldn't tell anyone. And I tried to recall just why it was he was so scared of being discovered. I knew it was illegal for Davey and his family to live in the camps, but they'd surely be found out eventually. So maybe Davey was just staying for a while, until his dad and brother got there. Then what? If I tried to think it all through too much, it didn't make sense. The only thing I felt certain of was that Davey was still out there alone and probably needing more help than ever.

Between being worried over Davey and stuck helplessly in

my house, it was torture. And there was no one I could talk to about it. I reminded myself that the storm would pass and I could race out there and check on him as soon as it did.

Stay there and hang on, Davey . . . Just hang on.

The skies finally cleared that evening, but it was too late to go into the swamp. At the dinner table that night I told Dad that I wanted to get up early and go fishing.

"I think we're all getting a little stir-crazy," he said. "You need me to help you get the boat down before I leave for work?"

"No, sir. I can do it. And I might leave before daylight. Before you get up. You said the fish bite best at sunrise."

Mom looked at him. "Is that safe, Roger?" she said.

"You test the navigation lights?" he asked me.

"Yes, sir. They work."

He looked at Mom. "He'll be fine. He needs to practice running in the dark sooner or later, and it's better when the sun's about to come up than go down."

I could see by Mom's expression that she didn't fully agree, but she just raised her eyebrows and didn't say anything.

Dad saw she wasn't going to object and turned back to me. "Just take it slow, son. Make sure you wear the kill-switch lanyard on your wrist."

I nodded, trying not to appear too eager.

I woke before daybreak, grabbed my pack, and stuffed a towel into it. Then I walked through our quiet house into the kitchen. I took a few more cans of food and filled a plastic milk jug with water. I couldn't remember the last time I'd gotten up before Dad, and I kept looking around like he'd appear behind me at any minute.

The air was thick and heavy, and a thin layer of fog lay over the swollen bayou. I let the *Bream Chaser* down and loaded my fishing rod and pack. Then I got into it, put on my flotation vest, and pulled the knob for the navigation lights. The single green and red bulbs on the bow came on, and I turned and saw the white stern light working as well. Then I put on the wristband that attached to the kill switch by a cord, which would disconnect the switch and cut the engine if I went overboard. I cranked the motor and sputtered out into the fog.

The waterway was eerie and exciting. I traveled slowly, occasionally looking up at the trees to make sure I was in the middle of the creek. Once I built my confidence, I sped up until the *Bream Chaser* was cutting smoothly through the dark water.

I slowed at the mouth of the river. The fog had thinned, and the sun bled cool red through the tops of the swamp trees; overhead the sky was cloudless. The water before me was swift and heavy with floating logs and tree branches. I sped up again and made my way upriver through the storm debris.

It took me nearly a half hour to make it to the mouth of Ware Bayou. I slowed to idle speed, swung wide of the dead-head, and sped up again. I hadn't gone far before I saw the canoe sunk to the gunnels and lodged under a cypress branch. I stopped and called for Davey, thinking maybe he was nearby. There was no answer, and I saw nothing to indicate a trail that he would have taken into the swamp. I wondered if the canoe had drifted there with the floodwater and filled with rain. Then I had a horrible thought.

Davey tried to leave. And didn't make it.

"Davey," I called once more. Again there was nothing but the silent swamp.

I grabbed a small piece of rope tied to the bow of the canoe and fastened it to the stern of the *Bream Chaser.* Then I motored slowly the rest of the way, towing it behind. When the camp came into view I saw the two catfish jugs drifting against the creek bank. But I didn't see Davey waiting for me as he usually did. I expected him to have heard me and already be standing on the deck, watching with that excitement in his eyes.

As I came closer I saw the grill outside. Several pieces of scrap wood and wet newspaper lay next to it. The remaining windowpanes of the camp were pasted with leaves, and a few branches lay on the roof. Otherwise, it looked intact and was leaning no more than it ever had. Then my eyes wandered down to a small mound before the grill. In a moment I realized it was Davey, lying there in his same clothes with his knees pulled up against his chest. His glasses were gone and his eyes were watching me. They had a tender, dulled look to them.

"Davey?" I said.

He blinked.

I pulled up to the dock and got out, looping my line around the nail. I stepped onto the deck and knelt before him.

"Davey?" I said again.

He cocked his eyes at me.

"Are you okay?"

He shivered and pulled his knees tighter.

"Davey, are you sick?"

He didn't say anything.

"Hold on," I said.

I went back to the *Bream Chaser* and returned with my pack. I took the towel out of it. Then I helped him sit up and put it around his shoulders. He was stiff and trembling.

"I found your canoe."

He nodded weakly.

"You need to get dry," I said. "What'd you do, lie out here in the storm?"

"I stayed inside, mostly," he muttered, staring at the deck.

I pulled the towel tighter around his shoulders, then glanced at the grill. "Have you eaten anything?"

He shook his head.

"Why haven't you eaten anything?"

He looked up at me. Tears were running down his face. "They didn't come," he said.

14

I DIDN'T KNOW WHAT TO TELL DAVEY TO MAKE
him feel better.

"You have to eat," I said.

"I tried to start a fire this morning. Everything's wet."

"Why didn't you take the grill inside?"

"Everything's wet," he said again.

"Your sheets, too?"

He nodded.

"All right," I said, thinking. "I brought some chicken noodle soup. I'll open it and you can drink it cold."

"Why didn't they come?" he said.

The soup can had a pull-tab lid, so I didn't need any tool
to open it.

"Sam?" he pleaded.

"I don't know," I said. "I don't know why they didn't come."

I took the soup and put it up to his mouth and tilted it. He
took a small swallow.

"Come on, Davey. You've gotta eat more than that."

He pushed my hand away and lay on his side again.

I set the can down. "What are you gonna do, die out here?"

He blinked and didn't answer.

"I'm gonna take you to my parents' house," I said. "This is crazy."

Davey suddenly sat up and scooted against the wall and stared at me like I was threatening his life.

"I'm not goin' back," he said.

"It's just my parents. What are you so scared of?"

"Somebody'll put me in another foster home."

Now I was even more confused.

"If you have a dad, then why were you in a foster home?"

"He went to jail at Parchman," Davey said.

"For what?"

"He got in a fight with somebody," he said. "But now he's out."

"So why would they send you to another foster home?"

Davey didn't answer me right away. "I don't know," he finally said. "But they might."

Then I understood. "Because maybe your dad isn't coming for you?"

"He is, too," Davey insisted. "Slade said he was."

"Who's Slade?"

"My brother." Davey looked at the floor again. "It was awful where I lived."

"It can't have been worse than this."

He looked at me again. "It was."

I didn't say anything.

"I just want my family," Davey said.

"But you can't stay out here if they don't come."

"I'll drown myself before I go back."

"Don't talk like that."

"Somebody told me drowning doesn't hurt."

"*I'm* here, Davey. You're not alone."

"But you'll leave me like you did before."

"I came back."

"But you'll leave again."

I took a deep breath. "I think you're just lonely," I said. "And the storm was scary. Once your dad and brother show up, you won't be talking crazy."

Davey looked at the floor.

"Where are your glasses?" I asked.

He shrugged.

I got up and went into the camp. Two sheets of tin were missing from directly over the bunks. The floor was still damp and soft, and the walls had wet streaks down them. I saw the sheets and pillow balled up on the bottom bunk. The mattress on the top bunk was wet as a sponge and smelled awful. I walked over to Baldy's pot on the counter. The eyedropper and the open pill bottle lay beside it. I poked around in the stuffing until I felt the baby mouse, stiff and dead.

I saw Davey's glasses on the floor. I picked them up and brought them outside and knelt before him. I decided not to tell him about Baldy, although I figured he probably knew.

"No wonder you got so wet," I said, "with part of the roof missing."

Davey kept staring at the floor.

"Here," I said, slipping the glasses on his face.

He looked at me and his eyes appeared slightly bigger and the old Davey was back.

"That better?"

He sniffled and didn't answer.

"What happened?"

"I started to fix it. Then I couldn't get the new tin up."

"I'll stay here with you this morning," I said. "Then I have to go home for lunch. I'll come back as soon as I can."

"Today?"

"Yes, today."

"What about tonight?"

"What do you mean, tonight?"

"Stay here with me."

"I can't stay here," I said.

Davey looked at the floor again. Suddenly there was nothing I wanted more than to stay out there with him.

"I'll see if I can figure something out," I said.

He looked up again. "Really?"

"I'll *see*. But I don't know how I can pull it off."

You'd have thought I'd said yes by the excitement in his eyes.

"Let's just eat right now," I said.

"Okay," he said.

I gave him the soup can, and he brought it to his mouth and started drinking.

"Did you get *anything* done while I was gone?"

"I put some of the boards down."

I looked at the deck and saw a few of the rotten planks had been replaced.

"What about your catfish jugs?" I said. "They're all in the weeds."

"It just rained so much," he said. "And it was cold."

I stood. "I'll get your sheets and pillow and bring them out to dry in the sun. Then we'll pick up the trash and get your fishing jugs working again. That should make you feel better."

Davey set the soup can down and looked up at me. "Did you tell your parents about me?"

I shook my head. "No. I told you I wouldn't. Now, come on. Let's clean this place up."

"We need to bury Baldy," he said.

"Yeah," I said. "I know."

15

I DUG A LITTLE HOLE BENEATH THE CAMP AND
Davey passed the cooking pot to me. I put Baldy into the hole
and covered him.

"You can probably find another mouse," I said.

Davey nodded. I started to climb back onto the deck when
I noticed a footpath leading out into the swamp.

"Did you make this trail?" I asked.

"What trail?"

I pointed to the pressed grass leading through the vines
and palmettos.

"No," he said. "Slade must have."

"I thought he didn't come."

"Before I came. He was out here for a while."

"Have you followed it?"

He shook his head. "It's just a lot of muddy ground.
Maybe he took some trash back there."

I studied the trail for a moment longer, then climbed back
onto the deck with Baldy's old pot. We spent the rest of the
morning cleaning the camp and getting everything in order

again. We pulled the wet mattress off the top bunk and dragged it outside. It would never dry enough to burn, so we rolled it off the deck into the marsh. Then I helped Davey collect more firewood and re-bait the catfish jugs. By the time I had to leave he'd regained a little of his spirit.

"You better bring a pillow for yourself when you come back," he said. "I've only got the one."

I sighed at the situation I felt myself falling into. "I really don't know how I can do this, Davey. My parents don't want me coming out here at all, much less spending the night."

"I need you to," he said.

I stepped into the *Bream Chaser* and breathed deep through my nose. "I'll be back in a couple of hours."

"With another pillow."

"Okay! With another pillow . . . Geez."

Davey smiled.

On the way home my mind raced with ideas of how I could pull off a night in the swamp with Davey. The obvious solution was to tell my parents I was staying over at Grover's. There was always the risk they would call his house, but that wasn't likely. Staying at the Middletons' had become so routine that they didn't usually check on me.

As it turned out, things weren't going to be as easy as I thought. When I got home I was surprised to walk into our house and see Dad. He told me was taking the afternoon off to work on his boat. I soon found myself sitting at the table with my parents, picking at a piece of fried chicken. I hadn't expected to have to lie to both of them.

"Son, did you move that stack of scrap lumber I had out back?" Dad asked me.

I'd forgotten all about it. "Yes, sir," I said. "I took it to build something with."

"Build something. Really? Is that where my saw and hammer went?"

I nodded.

"Build what?" he continued.

"Just a platform," I lied. "A swim platform."

"Where?"

"Near Grover's house. He asked if I could sleep over again tonight," I added.

"I suppose that's fine," Mom said. "What time will you be back?"

"You know, before lunch."

"Maybe you can get Grover out of the basement and take him fishing," Dad said.

"That's what I was thinking," I said.

After we finished eating, Dad went outside to wash his boat. It had been sitting on a trailer in our yard since the end of last summer, and he was getting it ready to put in the water again. He'd already ordered the lumber for another boat lift.

I got my plate and started for the kitchen. I walked around Mom and put the plate in the sink and continued as calmly as I could to the garage. I got another lawn bag and dropped a couple of Dad's shop towels into it. Then I returned to my room and stuffed my pillow and a few extra clothes on top. As I tried to slip through the kitchen unnoticed, Mom stopped me.

"Seriously, Sam? You can't go over to the Middletons' hauling a garbage bag. What do you have in there?"

My heart started racing. Mom can sniff out an iffy situation like a bloodhound.

"My pillow and pajamas," I said. "And some things I borrowed from Grover. So they don't get wet."

Mom studied the bag. "Please, leave the bag in the boat when you get there."

"Okay," I said, hurrying away.

"And make good decisions," she said.

"I will," I said. "See you tomorrow."

I went out the back door, the lawn bag slung over my shoulder. I hurried to the *Bream Chaser*, relieved that Dad was still in the driveway and wasn't there to question me any further. A moment later I was racing along the bayou toward the swamp.

Deep down, I knew there was no way I'd ever get away with it.

16

I DUMPED THE CONTENTS OF THE LAWN BAG ON the deck, and Davey smiled.

"You're really gonna stay?" he said.

"Yeah," I said reluctantly. "But only for one night. We've got to figure out what you're gonna do before I leave tomorrow."

Davey didn't seem to care about tomorrow. "I caught another fish while you were gone," he said.

"Great," I said. I pointed to the pile of clothes. "There's some clean clothes you can change into."

"I feel okay now," he said.

"Well, you still look like you've been rolling around in the mud."

"I'll give 'em back to you," he said.

"Don't worry about it," I said. "Get changed, and then we'll put some new tin over that giant hole in the roof."

While Davey changed into fresh clothes I went inside to spread the sheets on the bunks. The camp already smelled better with the wet mattress gone, and it felt better after drying in the sun all day. After a moment Davey came inside and stood there smiling like he thought there was something funny about wearing my clothes.

"You look fine," I said.

"Same size," he said.

"They're a little big, but that's okay."

"You take the bottom bunk with the mattress," he said.

"I'm fine on the boards."

"I'm scared on the bottom," he said.

"No wonder you got so wet."

Davey didn't answer. He kept watching me like I was supposed to tell him everything to do.

"How'd you get onto the roof?" I asked.

Davey led me outside and showed me the tree he'd climbed. I got the hammer and nails and started up. In a moment I was standing on top of the roof, terrified. It wasn't just the height—the tin was so rusty and the beams so rotten I was worried I'd fall through at any moment. From below, Davey slid me two sheets of the salvaged tin he'd brought from one of the other camps. I laid them over the hole and quickly hammered them down.

Once the roof was repaired I climbed down again and stood on the deck, feeling I'd narrowly escaped injury.

"What do you wanna do next?" Davey asked, like I had all the ideas.

I wiped the sweat from my forehead. "How many fish have you got on the stringer?"

"Just one. I had some more, but they died."

"Maybe we can get another one before dark."

"We can sit outside and watch the jugs. You can tell when there's a fish on there. It starts movin' around."

Taking a break sounded good. "All right," I said. "Let's go watch."

We sat on the edge of the deck, our feet hanging over the marsh grass. The jugs sat motionless on the black creek water.

"So have you thought about what you're gonna do?" I asked. "If your family doesn't come, I mean."

"They'll come," he said.

"You didn't seem so sure this morning."

"I feel better about it now."

"Don't you think they would have at least checked on you?"

Davey didn't answer me right away. "I think one of the jugs moved," he finally said.

I glanced at the creek. The jugs hadn't moved at all.

"Davey, you have to think about what you'll do if they don't show. You'll have to come with me."

"I won't go back," he said stubbornly.

"What if you could get another foster home?"

"I don't need another one. I'm gonna live with my dad."

"What does your dad do, now that he's out of jail? What's his name? Maybe I can find him for you. Find out where he is. Maybe something happened to him. My dad's a policeman, and he can find just about anybody."

Suddenly Davey looked at me. "He's a policeman?"

"Yeah."

Davey began breathing hard.

"Hey," I said, "it's not like that. He'll help you. He won't make you go somewhere you don't want to."

"Y-you can't tell him about me," he stammered.

"Okay, I won't tell him about you. Geez, it's okay."

Davey stared at the water.

"I can get on the Internet," I said. "I can look for your dad myself."

Davey nodded and appeared to calm down.

"So tell me about him," I said.

"His name's John Wilcox. But he just got out of jail, and only Slade knows where he is."

"So where is Slade?"

"I think the jug moved," Davey said.

"No it didn't."

"Yes it did."

"No it *didn't*," I said.

Davey stared at the jug a moment longer. "I don't know where Slade is," he said. "He told me he had some stuff to do."

"Maybe something happened to him?"

Davey suddenly got up and went into the camp while I stayed there, growing frustrated.

"You won't even listen to me," I said. "And you won't let me help you."

Davey didn't answer.

"Why'd you even ask me to come here?" I said over my shoulder. "I could get in a lot of trouble over this, you know."

I heard Davey moving something across the floor on the other side of the wall.

"My parents might have already called my friend's house and found out I'm not there," I said.

The camp grew quiet.

"I told you everything I know," Davey said behind me.

I turned and looked up at him. He was holding out a plastic sack. I took it from him and studied it.

"What's in there?"

"You can have it for the boards and the food, and for me gettin' you in trouble . . . I don't need it."

I opened the bag and saw that it was stuffed full of money. There must have been thousands of dollars in there.

17

THE SUN WAS STARTING TO FALL BELOW THE
treetops, and the air was turning chilly. I stared at the money
in disbelief. I'd never seen so much in my life. The first thing
I thought of was Officer Stockton telling me about the robbery at the fish market.

"Where'd you get that money?" I asked.

"Slade gave it to me."

"Where'd *he* get it?"

"I don't know. I guess he earned it."

"What kind of boat does he have?"

"He doesn't have a boat."

"Well, how did he get out here before?"

"His friend Jesse brought him. Jesse has a boat."

"What kind?"

"A pontoon boat."

I took a deep breath of relief.

"What?" Davey said.

"Nothing," I said. "But I can't take all this. I can't take
any of it."

"I don't need it," he said.

I set the bag down and stood up. "There's probably enough there to do whatever you want, Davey."

"I don't know how much it is."

I fought back the urge to dump the money out and count it. "Take it inside and put it back."

"But it's yours now."

I frowned. "Fine. Then go hide it for me."

Davey got the bag and went inside with it.

"I'll get a fire put together," I said, "so we have it to light when it gets dark. I've got some dry shop towels to burn, but I didn't have time to get more lumber."

"I've got somethin'," he called from inside.

I was putting the towels into the grill when he returned and held out pieces of a broken chair I remembered seeing in the corner. They looked dry enough.

"That'll work," I said, taking them from him.

"I've never had anybody spend the night over," he said.

"Seriously?"

"Dad went to jail when I was seven," he said.

I arranged the wood over the towels and thought about it. "That's a long time to be in jail for a fight."

"How long is it usually?"

"I don't know," I said. "But that's like . . . How old are you?"

"Twelve," he said.

"Yeah, he was in jail for five years. That's pretty long."

Davey laughed for the first time that I could remember. It was a funny, choppy laugh. "I'm not stupid," he said.

I laughed with him and shut the grill.

"No. I don't think you're stupid . . . just stubborn."

Davey smiled.

"You wanna go in your boat?" he asked. "You haven't taken me in your boat."

"Sure," I said. "We can go for a quick ride before it gets dark. And you can go swimming and clean up."

Davey sat on the front bench seat while I motored out of Ware Bayou and into the river. When I sped up he turned and looked at me with his wide grin. He started to stand, and I shouted over the engine noise for him to sit down. He did and looked back at me again, and he was laughing. Then he faced forward and held his hands up in the air, feeling the wind on his palms.

"You've never been in a boat before?" I shouted.

He shook his head. "Nothing fast. Just that canoe," he said. "This is awesome!"

"This one's really not that fast either," I said. "Dad's is way faster."

Davey looked back at me, the grin still frozen on his face.

I went about a quarter mile and circled back. When we

were at the creek again, I slowed in the middle and shut off the motor. The sun was low in the treetops, and the swamp was quiet and still, settled into a predusk lull. I took my T-shirt off and tossed it on the seat.

"You wanna swim here?" Davey asked.

I studied the water and the marsh grass at the edges, looking for alligators. I didn't think they'd attack us, but I was still uneasy with all the big ones I'd seen in the area.

"Sure," I said.

Davey pulled his shirt off and removed his glasses and wrapped them in it. Then he set the bundle on the seat and leaped in. He surfaced and grabbed the side of the *Bream Chaser* and hung there, watching me.

"You comin'?" he asked.

I slipped over the side and hung next to him. Even though I was nervous about alligators and whatever else might be in the dark depths under my feet, the water was cool and refreshing. I looked at Davey and laughed nervously. His face was still streaked with dirt and grime. I reached into the *Bream Chaser* and grabbed my shirt and gave it to him.

"Get it wet and rub your face," I said.

"I can use *my* shirt," he said. "The one you gave me."

"It's fine. Use mine. It'll dry."

Davey wet the shirt and started rubbing his face. In a moment he put the shirt back in the *Bream Chaser*, and when he turned to me he looked much better.

"You still lookin' for the dead body?" he asked.

"I wish you wouldn't talk about that while we're swimming."

Davey laughed his funny laugh.

"Not really," I said.

"It's not a big deal," he said. "You can tell there's nobody in there. Like their spirit got sucked away."

"You've seen one?"

Davey nodded. "My mom. In the coffin."

"Geez."

"It's not scary like you think," he said.

"Well, if I had one float up beside me right now with crabs all over it, I'd be scared."

Davey laughed again. "Yeah," he said. "Me too."

"But I've been working on being brave," I said.

"Then I've got an idea," he said.

Davey made up a game to test our bravery. We took turns swimming ten feet down to the bottom of the creek and bringing up handfuls of mud to prove we'd been there. The cool, murky depths were terrifying and thrilling at the same time. The mud was as black and stinky and gooey as tar. Then, out of nowhere, Davey got excited and tossed a clump of it at me, and it splatted on my forehead. I looked at him in disbelief, muck dripping down my face. I could tell by his expression he didn't know if I was going to get mad or laugh. I laughed, but mostly because he looked so funny and nervous about what he'd done. Then I lobbed some back at him, and that started the mud war. We spent nearly a half hour ambushing each other on different sides of the boat until we were coated with the stinky stuff and laughing until our sides hurt.

After the war we washed the mud from our hair and faces and climbed back into the *Bream Chaser*. When we finally started back to the camp the sun had set behind the trees and the creek was dark with cool shadow. The swamp was filled with the chatter of frogs and cicadas and crickets anticipating the darkness. Two alligators glided slowly across the surface, hunting for fish. I pulled the switch for the navigation lights and studied the waterway ahead. As we motored slowly through the cool, cheeping dusk, I sensed that now I was getting myself deeper into a kind of trouble that was a lot more complicated than a few lies. I was convinced that Davey really had told me all he knew, but somehow he seemed more strange and mysterious than ever.

18

WHEN WE GOT BACK TO CAMP THE MOSQUITOES
were out. Davey got the insect repellent, and we took turns
wiping it on ourselves. After we put our shirts back on, we lit
the fire and started cooking the fish. We stood before the grill,
mesmerized by the flames. Even with stars everywhere overhead, the swamp was darker and louder and spookier than I
expected. I couldn't even imagine spending a night alone there.

"You know," I said, "when your dad and brother show up,
they might not like this place the way it is."

"I was gonna get some more of that roofing tin from
those other camps."

"I can help you before I have to get back."

"Don't do that."

"What?"

"Talk about leavin'."

"You know I have to leave."

"Just don't talk about it."

"Okay," I said. "I won't."

We ate the fish with a can of green beans and passed the

jug of drinking water between us. When we were done I put more wood on the fire until the flames leaped above the lid and the light reached out to where we were sitting.

"There must be a million frogs out there," I said.

"Five million," Davey said.

"I hear there's bears out here," I said.

"I saw some wild pigs one day."

"Really?"

"Yeah. They came right behind the camp. About six."

"With tusks?"

"I don't know."

I remembered Davey's eyesight. "Probably hard to tell," I said. "But maybe that's what made the trail."

"Maybe," he said.

Later, when we went inside, Davey climbed up to his bed and I got onto the bottom bunk and pulled one side of the sheet over me to keep off the mosquitoes. I lay there feeling so far away from home that I could have been sleeping on the moon. It was especially hot and stuffy with the sheet over my face. I didn't see how I was going to sleep.

"Mosquitoes gettin' you?" he asked from above.

"No. You?"

"No. They're not gettin' me at all."

"Good," I said. "It's pretty hot, though."

Neither of us spoke for a moment.

"You know that canoe?" Davey said.

"Yeah."

"It used to be ours when we all lived in Escatawpa. Slade went and got it for me. I remember one time Daddy paddled me out here in it. All the way from the bridge. I was little, and he made me sit in the bottom in front of him and his knees came up over my shoulders. It seemed like it took a really long time, like all day. But I liked it. It was quiet and I could hear the birds, and the fish made swirls next to us."

"What's your dad like?"

"He's kind of short, like me. He has a jagged scar on his forehead where a dog bit him when he was my age. He said they didn't sew it up right. He always brushed his hair over it."

"What kind of dog?"

"A pit bull, I think."

I imagined a man version of Davey, with his bangs brushed straight down over his forehead.

"He said I talked a lot," Davey continued.

"Well, you kind of do. But not too much."

"Sometimes I want to know things," Davey said. "He always answered my questions."

"Sometimes my dad gets real quiet," I said. "Like he's thinking about a lot of things."

"Why are you workin' on being brave?"

I wasn't sure I wanted to talk about the fight. Davey was the first person I'd ever known who seemed to look up to me.

And it felt good. And I didn't want that feeling to go away. But then I realized that letting him look up to me was like a lie if he didn't really know me.

"You ever feel like you don't like yourself?" I said. "Like you want to change?"

"I've never thought about it."

"Never?"

"Well, I don't like the way things *are* sometimes. But I don't not like *myself* about it."

"I thought finding the dead body would make me brave. Like my dad. I wanna be more like him."

"Why?"

I struggled to tell him about the fight, but I couldn't do it. "I just want people to think I'm cool," I said.

"You're the coolest guy I've ever met."

"Well, doesn't sound like you've been around a lot of people."

"My brother's cool. Super cool. But he's older."

"Your dad must have gotten into a bad fight if he got sent to jail for five years."

"Yeah. My stepmom got a boyfriend, and Dad stabbed him in the stomach with a knife."

"Wow . . . Did he kill him?"

"No. Dad said he didn't mean to do it. He said sometimes you get so mad about things that you do stuff you didn't mean to do."

"I guess he would have gone to jail a lot longer if he'd killed him."

"Yeah," Davey said.

I rolled over on my side and stared across the floor at the open doorway. It was lighter outside than inside the camp, and I could see moonlight reflecting off the still creek. The sounds of the swamp pressed in on us from all directions.

"Davey," I said.

"What?"

"This is the most awesome thing I've ever done."

"Yeah," he said. "Me too."

19

I WOKE SATURDAY MORNING AS SUNBEAMS CAME through the window and fell across my sheet. The cheeping of the frogs had ceased, and it was still too early for insects to be buzzing. I uncovered my face and looked at the inside of the camp, amazed that I'd actually spent a night in the place. Out of the doorway I saw Davey on the creek in his canoe. He was pulling one of his jugs from the water, and I saw a large catfish flipping silvery in the light.

I climbed down from the bunk and walked onto the deck, rubbing my eyes. Davey looked across at me and held the fish up and smiled.

"Breakfast," he said.

Normally I wouldn't have cooked a catfish for breakfast, but at the time I couldn't think of anything I wanted more.

I took out the box of matches I'd brought and gathered a few pieces of paper and scrap lumber. By the time Davey arrived with the fish, I had a small curl of smoke coming from the fire.

"What time did you get up?" I asked him.

He sat beside me with his knife and began cleaning the fish. "I don't know," he said. "It was still dark."

I didn't know why it hadn't occurred to me before, but he didn't have a watch or any other way to tell time. I looked at my own watch. It was seven o'clock.

Davey stood with the headless, gutted catfish and studied the fire in the grill. I saw that the flames were taking, and I put the grate over it. He placed the fish on top.

"I need to bring spices," I said. "We could make it just like Mom does."

"Daddy used to have a generator," Davey said. "If we had a generator, we could get a microwave oven."

"And air conditioning," I said.

"And a radio," Davey said. "Think you can get us a generator?"

"There's no way!" I said.

Davey studied me with a "Why not?" look.

"Are you crazy? Even if I *could* sneak Dad's out of the garage, they weigh like a hundred pounds."

Davey shrugged.

I looked at the fish and shook my head. "Geez," I said.

"You've got plenty of money now," Davey said. "You could buy one for us."

"I'm not talking about that money anymore. I told you I don't want it."

"But wouldn't it be cool to have power?"

"Yes," I said. "It would."

"And we could stay out here and have everything we needed. Just like a real home."

It struck me that Davey was talking like his dad and brother weren't going to show up. I started to picture him living out here alone by himself. And as I stood there cooking the fish on the grill and thinking about getting an electric generator—it didn't seem all that impossible.

"How would you go to school if you lived out here?" I said. "You'd have to go to school."

"I just wouldn't," he said. "I'd just be gone from the world."

"Like people would think you were dead?"

"I don't know what they'd think. I'd just be gone."

I wanted to ask him again about his dad and brother, but now I understood why he didn't like me talking about leaving. I didn't want anything to change either.

"You could just be gone, too," he said softly.

I looked at Davey. I started to say something, but I didn't. I looked away again and grabbed the fork and turned the fish.

"You can like yourself here," he said.

Davey was right. I couldn't remember the last time I'd felt so good about myself. Even before the fight. But nothing in my life fit into this place. If I was going to stay, I would have to leave my parents and everything I knew behind. It seemed impossible.

"I *wish* I could stay out here," I said.

"Then do it," he said.

I turned to him again. "Are you giving up on your dad and your brother?"

Davey shrugged. "I don't know what could have happened."

"I guess if you're not leaving and they don't come, then you don't have a choice, do you?"

"No," he said.

"So it's easy for you. It's not easy for me."

Davey looked at the deck and nodded. And suddenly I was confused about everything again.

"Why wouldn't they come, Davey?"

He looked up at me.

"It doesn't make any sense," I said. "No dad would leave his son out here like this."

"Unless the dad didn't care about him," Davey said.

This was a different Davey from the one I'd known just a few days before. I'd never heard him be anything but optimistic.

"There's nothing wrong with you," I said.

"There's nothing wrong with you either. And *you* don't even like you."

I shook my head and looked at the fish again. I poked it with the fork and found that the meat was ready. I held out my free hand, and Davey gave me the knife. I used the two instruments to lift the fish from the grill and set it down on the deck. Then we sat on either side of it, and I peeled some of the smoking meat back to cool.

"I've got to go after we eat," I said.

"But you're coming back, right?"

I peeled some more of the meat away and stared at it. "I have to work some things out," I said.

"And then you'll be back."

"Yes," I said. "I'll bring some spices and maybe some cookies we can eat for dessert. I'll sleep on the top bunk if you want me to."

"No," he said. "The top bunk's fine. I'll be fine."

20

RIDING BACK, I FELT STRANGE. LIKE ALL MY LIFE there had been a big wall in front of me that I couldn't get past, and now I'd climbed to the top and jumped over and faced a land of stretching green meadows that was full of nothing but excitement and opportunity. And if I stayed there, none of the stuff on the other side of the wall behind me could ever get to me and be part of my life again.

But that wasn't really how it was.

Just because I walled it all away didn't mean it wasn't still there, in my head. Where it always was. Like fires burning in the distance.

Or, really, just one fire. And it wasn't the fight. I wasn't thinking about Leroy Parnell and Gooch at all.

That one fire was Grover. And maybe if I put it out—apologized to him—it would ease my guilt and make my new life as good as it *should* be. I didn't have to hang out with Grover anymore. I didn't have to be his best friend. If I just put out the fire, did the right thing, then I could walk away from the ashes with a clear conscience. Back to Davey and the swamp.

Where everything was perfect.

· · ·

When I got home Mom was at the church and the house was empty. She kept a pen and notepad next to the telephone in the kitchen to jot messages. She had left a message for me saying that she'd put some gumbo in the refrigerator and to leave word if I was staying over at Grover's again. I should have been relieved at how easy my parents were making it for me, but instead I walked through the empty house feeling guiltier than ever. I stared at old pictures of our family at the beach and Disney World, trying to remember those times. For some reason I think I wanted Mom to walk in the door. I wanted to see her, and maybe somehow she'd know something to tell me. But the clock on the fireplace mantel kept ticking in its lonely way, and I knew she wouldn't be back until later that afternoon.

I walked back into the kitchen, where I heated up some of the gumbo and ate it. Then I approached the notepad and picked up the pen. I forced the words.

> Spending the night at Grover's again.
> I'll ride to church with him. Thanks for the gumbo.
>
> Love, Sam

I pulled up to Grover's dock and tied the *Bream Chaser*. I glanced at my watch and saw that it was just before nine o'clock. I expected Grover was still asleep. I walked up his lawn and found the French doors to the back sitting room unlocked as usual. I entered the quiet house and crossed the floor to his lair. The door was cracked slightly, and I eased it open.

Something was immediately different about Grover's lair. At first I couldn't figure out just what it was. Then I realized the blackout shades were raised and the room was bright with sunlight. There was no trash lying about, and the blankets that were usually tangled and strewn across the floor in front of his television were neatly folded and draped over the backrest of the sofa. The bunk beds were made and empty. Grover wasn't there, and it didn't appear he'd been there at all recently.

I stood for a moment and studied the empty room, trying to get my head around it all. I looked at the staircase leading to the top floor of the Middletons' home. The only conclusion I could reach was that Grover was still sleeping, in his real room.

I crept upstairs and emerged in their large hallway. I was certain Dr. Middleton was at work, and it was likely that Mrs. Middleton was out of town. Natalia was certainly in the house somewhere, but probably at the other end, where the kitchen was. I turned right and started toward Grover's room. I found his door closed and I knocked softly.

No one answered.

I knocked again.

"Leave me alone, Natalia," Grover complained.

"It's me," I said.

Grover didn't answer. I turned the knob and pushed the door. I saw him lying in his bed with the blankets pulled up to his chin. He always slept like a mummy, with his hands straight down at his side. Nothing moved except his eyes. They were open and watching me.

"What do you want?" he said.

I crossed the floor and stood before his large antique, four-poster bed.

"What are you doing up here?" I said.

"Trying to sleep."

"What happened to the basement?"

"Nothing. It's still there."

"But it's all cleaned up. Like you haven't been down there."

Grover blinked and didn't move. "Maybe I haven't," he said. "What do you want?"

It struck me that my outburst at Grover had affected him more than I'd expected.

"Will you sit up so I can talk to you?"

Grover didn't move.

"What's wrong with you?"

"I just don't feel like getting up," he said.

I nodded. "Okay," I said.

"So what do you want?"

"I'm sorry about all that stuff I said. I didn't mean it."

"Yes you did."

"No I didn't."

Grover blinked again, then slowly eased out from under his blanket and leaned against the backboard of his bed. "Is that it?" he asked.

I was so tired of the lies. I just wanted them to stop, somehow. At least slow them down. "I told my parents I was spending the night over here," I said.

"Why?"

"Because I'm going to spend the night somewhere else. And they can't know about it."

"Where?"

"I can't tell anybody."

"You have new friends already?"

I swallowed nervously. "It's not like that," I said. "There's somebody who needs my help."

"Help with what?"

I hesitated. "I can't say."

"You think I would tell anybody?"

"No, I just promised I wouldn't talk about it."

"But it's okay to make me a liar, too?" Grover said.

"You don't have to have anything to do with it." It was a weak answer, but I couldn't think of any other way to put it.

Grover studied me for a moment. Then he got out of bed. "You make me need to pee," he said.

He went into his bathroom. After a moment I heard the toilet flush and he came back out and stood in front of me.

"I'm not doing you any more favors," he said.

"Fine," I said.

"The only reason I ever invited you over was because I felt sorry for you."

My old anger at Grover bubbled up as if it had been simmering all along.

"*You* felt sorry for *me*?" I said.

"Your dad's some redneck cop who built a piece-of-crap house, and your mom paints crappy pictures that nobody'll buy. Your whole life is crap, and it always will be."

In an instant I knew that everything I'd ever felt about Grover was right. And I felt like a fool for thinking I should apologize to him. The anger inside me boiled up into my throat and I couldn't hold it back. "My dad could kick your dad's ass if your dad was ever home!" I yelled.

Grover's face grew red and his cheeks began to twitch. I knew he was about to explode, and I wanted every bit of it. I'd never hated someone so much in my life.

"You wouldn't even come over here if your life wasn't such a suck-fest! Go back to your crappy boat and your crappy house and stop mooching off me!"

"I don't want anything of yours!"

"Then why are you here?"

"I don't know! I guess I made a mistake!"

"I guess you did," he said in a calm, mean way.

I was so mad my hands shook and my ears hummed. I turned and left. I don't remember walking downstairs and out the French doors. Before I knew it I was racing upriver, replaying all of Grover's words in my head.

21

FORGET YOU, GROVER.

The Pascagoula River curved away before me, silvery in the late-morning sun. The sky overhead was deep blue and cloudless. Spoonbill catfish broke the surface and rolled and disappeared into the depths again.

Loser.

A lone bull alligator crossed ahead of me, returning home after the morning hunt. The rains of the tropical storm were still draining from the swampland and the river. Though not as high as the day before, the waterway remained heavy with muddy water and sticks and leaves.

I did what I could. You can have your miserable life.

Gradually, the soothing vastness of the swamp overcame my foul mood, and everything behind me fell away again and ceased to matter. A bald eagle soared far overhead, and I wondered if Davey was watching it, too. Then it occurred to me that I didn't have the special spice mix my mom used on her catfish or any of the other things I had told him I would bring. But then I thought we didn't need it. We didn't need any of it.

When I arrived at the camp Davey was on the dock hammering down more of the loose planks. Most of them were too rotten to hold nails, but he looked up and smiled and I could tell he was enjoying himself.

By lunchtime we had two more catfish on the stringer Davey had tied to the end of the dock. We decided to save them until later and ate two cans of ravioli from the supplies I'd brought the day before. Then I boiled more drinking water while Davey swept out the camp and hammered a few more nails.

That afternoon we went riding in the *Bream Chaser* again, deep into the headwaters of Ware Bayou, where the water cleared and the channel became so narrow that Davey had to lift tree limbs for us to get through. The creek eventually ended in a marshy area with buggy whips and cattails higher than our heads.

"I'll bet tigers could live out here," Davey said.

"It looks like it," I said.

"I'll bet all kinds of things are out here that we don't even know about."

"I wish I knew more about plants we could eat."

"You can bring a book about it. We can try different things."

"If we could trap a hog, then we could get bacon."

"And steaks," he said.

"That's a cow," I said.

Davey laughed. "I wonder if there's wild cows out here."

The thought of it was funny. But then I remembered hearing about wild cows in Florida and, on the Discovery channel, seeing a different kind of wild cow in the Amazon or someplace like that.

"There's no telling," I said.

We turned around and made our way back to a wider part of the creek and went swimming. This time the water was only shoulder-deep and we could almost see our feet in the depths. Davey talked about getting more lumber from the old camps and building furniture and maybe even adding another room. He said if I could get books on farming and trap making, then he could get all the food we needed. From what I'd seen, he could barely drive a nail. I wasn't too optimistic about eating much more than what I could sneak away from home. But I'd never seen him so excited, and he made it all sound so good that I began to believe maybe we could really pull it off in some way.

As the swamp slipped into twilight the pulsing of the frogs and thrumming of the insects rose around us. I told Davey we'd better get back and start cooking the fish. We climbed into the *Bream Chaser*, and Davey positioned himself on the front seat, a smile still locked on his face as his imagination continued to work.

We cooked the fish and ate at our usual spot on the deck. The sky was so bright with stars that we could see without flashlights.

"I forgot the spice mix," I said.

"I like it fine," Davey said.

Then I thought about the reason I didn't have the spices or the cookies or anything else, and it made me stop chewing for a moment and fight the thought away.

"What's wrong?" Davey asked.

I started chewing again. "Nothing," I said.

"It's just old stuff," he said.

"Yeah," I said.

Davey smiled again and picked more fish off the board. I watched him and wondered how he could just forget everything when it seemed like he had a lot more problems behind him than I did. And I thought maybe if I just knew more about it all, it would help me.

"Will you tell me about the foster home?" I said.

Davey stopped smiling and looked up at me. His face was totally empty of expression. I immediately regretted the question.

"You don't have to," I said.

"No," he said, "but I will."

"It doesn't matter," I said.

"Yes it does."

I nodded.

"After I do, then you have to tell me why you don't like yourself," he said.

I took a deep breath through my nose and nodded.

"I never told anybody," Davey said.

"All right," I said. "I won't tell anybody else."

"My old foster home was in Moss Point. Dad got Slade to sneak me off in the night so we could be together again when he got out of prison."

"What was so bad about the foster home?"

"My foster dad used to tell me I was like a stray dog that nobody wanted. He hurt me sometimes, but he didn't do it so you could tell. He'd do things like press his thumbs up real hard under my armpits. I'd see his jaw get tight, like he might punch them all the way through. If I yelled, he'd press harder until I got quiet. It didn't leave any marks for the social services lady to see."

"Why'd he do it?"

"I don't know. I tried to help him and did the best I could. He had a dog kennel, and he'd keep people's dogs for 'em. He told everybody I was homeschooled, but I just looked after the dogs while he went out and did things. But I like dogs, so I tried to do a good job. I knew all their names and everything, even if I'd just seen 'em once. I'm good at dog names. But sometimes when he was around I'd spill some food or take too long with somethin'. He'd lose his temper real quick."

Davey took off his glasses and studied me.

"You see anything wrong?" he asked.

"Like what?"

"In my eyes."

I shook my head.

"I know. He got mad one day and sprayed me in the face with some air freshener. Everything's been blurry ever since. But you can't see anything wrong. The glasses don't really help much."

"Why didn't you tell somebody?"

Davey shrugged. "What if the next foster home was worse?"

"People don't do stuff like that," I said. "Not most people."

Davey slid his glasses back on. "I figure I'd rather have my own family or no family at all," he said.

"*Geez,*" I said. "That's a lot worse than mine. I just got beat up really bad one time by these two big guys at school. And I lost my . . . I lost a friend."

"He died?"

"No. I mean we just stopped being friends."

"How come?"

"Because he made me feel bad about myself."

"What did he do?"

"He just . . . People make fun of him, and I feel like they make fun of me because I'm friends with him. And I just don't want it to be like that anymore."

"Is he sad about it?"

"Well, I thought he was, but then he got really pissed

at me. Now I don't think he cares. I don't think he ever did."

Davey studied me.

"I think about that fight a lot. I think about this girl everybody likes. She saw it all happen."

"What's her name?"

"Julia."

"She's really pretty?"

"Yeah," I said. "She is."

Davey didn't say anything. And I suddenly felt how stupid my problems must sound compared to what he'd been through.

"So that's all it is," I said. "And it's just a bunch of stuff that's over now. That I'm trying not to think about anymore."

"It's easy to forget about it out here," Davey said. "Like a new life."

"I know," I said.

"But sometimes when I go to sleep I have the same dream, though I really don't know if it's the same dream or if the dream makes me think it is. So I wanna tell you about it, and if I have it again you can let me know," Davey hesitated.

"What?" I said.

"I'm in my canoe paddlin' on the river. It's night and I'm alone and the moon is shinin' on the water so I can see a long way in front of me and behind me. I'm paddlin' as fast as I can because every time I turn around I think I see another canoe far away behind me. It's just a little black speck, but I can tell they're movin' because I see the water turn white when they dip their paddle. It's scary because I know there shouldn't be anybody else out there. And I know they're comin' after me."

That night I had my own dream: I was putting the jugs out in the creek. I was alone. For some reason Davey had left long ago and it wasn't clear why. I decided to go home and get more supplies. When I arrived at my house Grover was on the dock with Dad. They were working together on a new boat lift. Dad had a beard, and both of them looked at me like they didn't know me.

"It's me," I said. "It's Sam."

They turned away and went back to their work like Grover was his new son.

"Remember?" I said. "You gave me this boat, Dad. The *Bream Chaser*."

"Sam doesn't live here anymore," Dad said over his shoulder.

I woke with a start. I lay there for a moment, remembering where I was. Night sounds pulsed in my ears and fear pounded in my chest.

"Sam!" I heard Davey yell.

I leaped from my sleeping bag and rushed outside. I found him standing on the deck, staring into the darkness.

"What is it?" I said.

"Hear that?" he shouted. "It's my brother, Slade!"

22

FIRST I HEARD VOICES IN THE DARKNESS. THEN I looked down the creek and saw the silhouette of someone standing on the bow of a boat, poling toward us.

"Slade!" Davey shouted.

"I'm comin'!" yelled the person on the boat. "Just hold on."

The boat drew closer and the person on the front pulled the pole from the water and tossed it behind him, where it banged onto the hull.

"Crap, Slade!" someone said. "Watch out, man!"

"Will you just shut up?" Slade replied. "I don't see you helpin' any."

The boat drifted to the dock, and Davey was already down there to help. Under the faint sky glow I studied his older brother. He had his shirt off and his chest heaved and glistened with sweat. He appeared to be about eighteen, thin and muscled, and not overly tall. He wore a braided ponytail down his back with a few strands of hair hanging over his eyes.

Davey sat at the edge of the dock and put his feet out to catch the boat as it came to rest next to mine.

"Where'd you get the boat?" Davey asked.

Slade used a finger to pull the hair out of his eyes and over his ear. I noticed his face was strangely round and fleshy, like a doll's. He didn't look anything like Davey.

"Doesn't matter," Slade said. "It's a piece of junk we're havin' to use because Jesse's motor went out on him."

Slade stepped onto the dock, and the two other boys with him stood up and made their way forward. Davey grabbed the bowline and wrapped it around a board, so excited that he could barely control his fingers.

"I thought you weren't comin'," Davey said.

"I almost didn't," Slade said. "We broke down a mile back." He turned to the other two. "Jesse, get the beer," he said.

"Is this the place?" one of the boys asked.

"No," Slade said sarcastically. "This is just a hotel I decided to stop at. What do you think, dumbass?"

Davey stood and looked up at his brother. Slade had his back to him, studying the camp.

"What took you so long?" Davey said.

Slade didn't answer him. His hair had fallen back over his face, and he fingered it behind his ear again. "What all'd you get done?" he asked.

"I cleaned it up and I hammered some of the loose boards," Davey said. "I fixed the rafters and I was gonna finish the roof next, but I needed some help. I did part of it."

Slade kept looking the camp over.

"Where's Dad?" Davey asked.

Slade hesitated. "He hasn't made it yet," he mumbled.

I immediately thought it was strange how he said it. Like he didn't want to talk about their dad for some reason. Then I realized Slade was more interested in me. He was turned back from the camp and staring at me.

"Who is this?" he said.

"He's my friend," Davey answered. "His name is Sam."

Slade turned and looked down at Davey. "What'd I tell you?"

Davey hesitated. "He's been helpin' me," he said. "He found me out here. And I didn't know—"

"Helpin' you? Then why ain't the roof done? You been out here for two weeks."

Davey looked down at the deck.

"What happened to your shoes?" Slade said.

"I don't have any," Davey mumbled.

"What?" Slade snapped.

"I don't have any," Davey said quietly. "You said you'd bring me what I needed."

Slade spit. "Crap," he said.

The other two boys came onto the dock carrying an ice cooler between them. One of them was about Slade's size, and the other was shorter and heavier.

Slade moved out of the way and motioned for them to

pass. "Take it up there, Jesse," he said to the thinner one. Then he turned to the heavier friend. "Fred, you got the flashlight?"

"Yeah," Fred said.

"I got one," Davey said, rushing past them.

I backed away as Slade's friends stepped onto the deck and set the cooler down.

"These boards gonna hold?" Jesse asked.

Davey came back with a light and shone it at their feet. "I put some new ones down."

Slade said, "Gimme the light, Fred."

Fred gave him a flashlight from his pocket, and Slade clicked it on and passed it over the deck. He frowned and then he shone it at the walls and up to the roof.

"How are we supposed to stay in this place?" Jesse said. "It looks like it's gonna collapse."

"We've been walkin' on the dock," Davey said nervously. "I think most of the floor's okay."

"It's been here for years," Fred said. "It's fine."

Slade took a deep breath and looked at Davey. "Just go get our sleepin' bags and those chairs we got in the boat. You can get your friend to help."

I went past the three boys and joined Davey on the dock. We got into the boat and found three sleeping bags and two foldout chairs and brought them up. Jesse and Fred were each drinking a beer when they took the chairs from us and sat before the cooler. Then we continued into the camp with the sleeping bags.

Slade was inside, shining his flashlight around. "You've been here two weeks and you couldn't clean it up any better?" he said.

Davey hung his head and didn't respond as we stood there holding the bags. After a moment Slade put his light in my face, then swung it to Davey's.

"I ain't sleepin' on the floor," he said. "Get your stuff off the beds and put it down here. Then put two of those bags on the bunks."

Davey didn't move.

"Come on, Davey," I said.

"Then go back to sleep," Slade added.

We got our sheets and piled them on the floor. Then we arranged two of the sleeping bags on the beds and left the third on the bottom bunk. We dragged our sheets near the kitchen counter and lay down on our backs. I heard Davey breathing hard next to me.

"It's okay," I said.

"But we did a lot," he said.

"We can do more in the morning."

"I wish Daddy were here," he said.

"You can find out where he is tomorrow."

"I thought Slade would like it," Davey said.

I didn't know what to say. I was just as confused as he was.

• • •

I lay awake listening to Davey breathing beside me. Now I wasn't just hot, but the floor was hard and hurt my back. The older boys stayed on the deck, drinking beer and talking quietly. After a while I needed to pee, but I didn't want to go out there with them. Then I knew I'd never get to sleep if I didn't go, so I got up and walked outside and stood behind them and started peeing into the marsh. I noticed they stopped talking, but I didn't want to look back. When I was done I sensed someone behind me. I turned and saw Slade's weird doll face inches from my own. The smell of beer and sweat fell over me, hot and putrid.

"What are you doin' out here?" he said in a way that scared me.

"I had to go," I said.

"I mean at our camp."

"Just helping Davey . . . like he told you. That's all."

"What'd he say?"

"About what?"

"About anything."

"Nothing. I mean, just that he was fixing up the camp and waiting for you and his dad."

"Who knows you're out here?"

I shook my head. "Nobody."

Slade studied me for what seemed like forever.

"Nobody knows I'm out here," I said again.

He continued to stare at me like there was no telling what he'd do. "And we're gonna keep it that way, right?" he finally said.

"Sure," I said. "Right."

"Where you from?"

"Kings Bayou," I said. "About a half hour—"

"I know where it is," Slade interrupted. He seemed to think about it for a moment. "What y'all been livin' on?"

"I've only been here a few times. Davey's had some fish. I brought him some canned food. But he hasn't been eating much."

"Why not?"

"I think he was lonely."

Slade backed away from me and looked over the creek. "Lord," he said.

"What'd you expect, Slade?" Jesse said. "He's only a kid."

Slade turned to him. "What am I supposed to do about it?"

"He's been out here alone for two *weeks*," Jesse said.

"I told you I can handle it," Slade snapped. "Who's in charge of the plan here?"

Jesse frowned and looked at his beer. "You are," he said.

"So don't complain if you want any part of it."

Jesse shook his head.

"What?" Slade challenged.

"It's just not exactly goin' smooth, is all."

"Yeah, and what about your life was so smooth before?"

"Hey," Fred interrupted, "we're good."

Slade kept staring at Jesse.

After a moment Jesse looked up at him. "Yeah, we're good, Slade. Relax, will you?"

Slade continued watching him until he looked away again. Then he turned back to me. "What are you lookin' at?"

"Nothing," I said.

"Go back to sleep."

I went into the camp and lay down next to Davey. I felt myself trembling. It was too dark to see if Davey was awake or not. If he'd heard what went on outside, he wasn't talking about it.

I didn't sleep well the rest of the night. The boys stayed outside drinking beer and smoking cigarettes and talking in their low tones. I couldn't make out all of what they were saying, but some of it was about money and a hardware store and a truck they had parked somewhere along the river.

Eventually dawn crept over the swamp and I began to see the tops of the trees across the creek framed in the dark hole of the camp door. The boys began to move about, and I heard the cooler sloshing with ice water. Then I heard them getting into the boat. A moment later the engine started and the sound of the motor faded away down the creek.

I lay there for a moment wondering how they'd fixed their motor all of a sudden. Then I was flooded with an awful realization. I got up and went to the door and looked out. The *Bream Chaser* was gone.

23

I RUSHED INTO THE CAMP AND STOOD OVER DAVEY, shouting his name.

He turned his head and looked at me.

"They took my boat!"

He sat up and stared out the door like he might see it.

"What am I going to do?" I said. "I've got to go home! I have to be back in time for church!"

He stood and walked outside and looked down the creek. "Why'd they take it?"

"I don't know! They just got in it and left. They didn't ask me or anything."

He looked over at the boat Slade and the others had come in last night. For the first time I studied it closely. It was a beat-up aluminum work boat that looked like some I'd seen tied up to tugs and construction barges. It was sixteen or eighteen feet long. Just like the one Officer Stockton had described.

"Think you can get that one workin'?" Davey said.

"I don't know anything about fixing engines! And what am I going to tell Dad?"

He turned to me. "Maybe they won't be gone long."

I took a deep breath. "Something's not right about all this, Davey."

He looked at the deck. "I wish my dad would come," he said.

"Slade doesn't even look like you."

"He's my stepbrother."

"So he's not even your real brother?"

"He's still my real brother."

"What did he say y'all were going to do out here?"

"He said we'd live in the camp."

I felt suddenly foolish and angry for entertaining Davey's fantasy of a life in the swamp.

"People can't live in this!" I said. "Don't you understand that? Even if it was fixed up, nobody lives out here!"

"That's what he promised," Davey said quietly.

"Well, he's not telling you everything. There's something else going on."

Davey started shaking. "He said to bring the money out here and fix it up so we could stay."

"Where'd he get all that money?"

"I don't know. He just gave it to me after he picked me up from my foster home."

"Who are his friends? Do you know anything about them?"

Davey shook his head.

"Slade is dangerous, Davey. Did you hear the way he talked to me last night?"

Davey shook his head again, but I could see he was hiding something.

"I thought he was going to hit me," I said.

Davey sat on the deck and pulled his knees up to his chest and stared at his kneecaps. "He wouldn't do that," he said.

"Well, he acted like it."

Davey didn't answer.

"Hey," I said.

He cocked his eyes up, and I realized the more angry I acted toward him the less help he'd be.

"I'll think of something," I said. "I'll find a can of food we can eat for breakfast. Then I'll look at that boat and see if I can get it started."

"Then you'll leave," he mumbled.

"I don't know what I'm gonna do. But if I don't figure out a way to get home, there's gonna be people all over the place looking for me."

Davey and I sat on the deck and ate cold chicken noodle soup from the can for breakfast. Afterward I climbed into the work boat and tried to crank it while Davey watched from above. The engine turned over, but the motor wouldn't start up. I didn't see a gas tank, so I assumed it was built into the seat. I searched until I found the fuel gauge near the key and saw that it was on empty.

"It's just out of gas," I said.

"Maybe they went to get some more," Davey said.

"Well, that doesn't help *me* any."

"What about the canoe?" Davey said.

"It'd take me hours to get back in that thing. I have to be back before church starts."

Davey began to rock again.

"I think he might have stolen that money," I said.

"Sometimes Slade steals things," Davey admitted.

"Geez," I said. "Has he gotten arrested before?"

Davey nodded against his knees.

"What's he gonna think about my dad being a policeman?"

"You better not tell him."

I sighed, feeling the weight of hopelessness settling on top of me.

"I don't know what to do, Davey."

"I think we should keep workin' on the camp," he said. "He might be mad if we don't."

"Davey, I think we both need to leave as soon as we find a way."

He shook his head.

"Why?" I said.

"My dad's gonna come."

"It doesn't look like it."

Davey didn't answer.

"You think he knows about Slade stealing money?"

"He wouldn't like it if he did. Dad doesn't do that sort of thing."

I didn't know what to believe anymore. What to care about. Davey's reasoning seemed to go in circles.

He looked at me. "Please, just help me fix somethin'. Until they get back."

I helped Davey nail some of the wall siding that was coming loose. It seemed like pointless work, and I couldn't stop worrying about what was going to happen if Slade and his friends didn't show soon. I could see it all playing out in my head. Grover would show up at church without me. Mom would find out I'd never been over there. Then my whole tangle of lies would begin to unravel itself. She'd tell Dad, and he'd call Officer Stockton. There would be search and rescue vessels all over the rivers and Coast Guard choppers in the air. And there was nothing I could do about it except wait until they found me.

I looked at Davey hitting the nails, his face twisted with concentration. *What did he think would happen then?*

But Davey didn't seem to think ahead at all.

24

SLADE AND THE BOYS MOTORED UP THE CREEK just after ten o'clock. I was doubtful, but I figured I might still have time to get home before Mom and Dad left for church. Then I could just ride with them and avoid Grover. I dropped the hammer and went down to the dock to catch the *Bream Chaser* while Davey watched.

My skiff looked close to sinking with the weight of all three of them balanced precariously in the center. Slade came in too fast, and I had to kick my feet out and turn the boat to keep it from slamming into the pilings. They were quiet and tired-looking, none of them talking. Jesse gave me the bow-line, and I took it and wrapped it around the nail and held the boat steady. Slade hefted the cooler onto the dock while Jesse crawled out with a jerrican of gasoline and Fred with a sack of McDonald's and another sack full of something. They stood on the dock and continued past me into the camp without a word.

Slade rubbed his eyes and looked up at Davey. "You get anything done?"

"We nailed some siding back on," Davey said. "Where'd you go?"

"Where do you think? You don't have anything to eat around here."

"We've got—"

"Nothing *we* want," Slade interrupted.

"I can catch fish."

"Well, go catch some, then. We've got McDonald's."

"I really can," Davey insisted.

Slade frowned and looked back at the *Bream Chaser.* "We almost sank in that thing," he said.

"My boat's not rated for that much weight," I said.

Slade glanced at me, then looked at Davey again.

"I'll get the fish," Davey said. He set down his hammer, jumped off into the marsh, went to his canoe, and began shoving it into the water.

Slade finally turned to me. "What?" he said.

"I need to go home."

Slade looked back at the creek. Davey was paddling across toward one of the jugs. Slade brushed the hair from his face and looked down at me.

"You remember that talk we had last night?"

"Yeah," I said.

He stared at me as if making sure.

"You live at 56 Acorn Drive?" he asked.

I swallowed. "Yeah. How'd you know?"

"It's in your boat. On the registration."

"Oh," I said.

He kept his eyes on me, and the fearsome weight of his doll face was heavy.

"So I know where you live," he said. "Don't forget that talk."

I felt my fingers trembling. "I won't tell anybody about your camp," I said.

"Good," he said.

He looked back at the *Bream Chaser*, studying it like he was making sure there wasn't anything else he needed from it. Then he turned and started toward the camp. It crossed my mind that he might not let me leave.

"Go ahead," he said over his shoulder. "Get out of here."

I knew I needed to leave quickly, but I felt I needed to say goodbye to Davey first. I motored across the creek to where he was working with the catfish jugs. I came up against the canoe, and he reached out and held my boat.

"You goin' home now?" he said.

"Yeah," I said.

Davey looked down and picked one of the jugs off the floor of the canoe and began to untangle it.

"Maybe your dad will be here soon," I said.

Davey nodded.

"And it looks like Slade and his friends got some things at the store. It shouldn't be so bad now."

Davey didn't look up. "I think if I show them I can catch fish, they'll like it better here," he said.

"Maybe so," I said.

Neither of us spoke for a moment. I knew what he wanted to ask me, but he didn't.

"So I better go," I said.

He looked up at me and nodded.

"You think you're going to be okay?" I asked.

He stared at me and nodded again, but I saw he wasn't sure at all.

"Bye," he said.

As I pulled away I should have been relieved, but I wasn't. It didn't seem right that it should all end so suddenly like this. And it was obvious that Davey wasn't going to be okay. But I was too concerned with getting home to dwell on it.

25

WHEN I GOT TO THE MOUTH OF WARE BAYOU I glanced down at my fuel tank, and the sight of the gauge set my heart to pounding in my chest again. They'd run it almost completely empty. It read less than one-eighth of a tank, and I'd never seen it that low before. I wasn't sure I could get even halfway home. If I ran out, then I'd have to wait for someone to come along and tow me—if there was anyone even close. And that would definitely blow any chance I had of getting back before Mom and Dad left for church.

I forced myself to stop thinking about the what-ifs and focus on my only course of action—getting as close to home as I could. I set my sights downriver and twisted the throttle.

I traveled close to the riverbank, where I could paddle the boat to land if I broke down. I remembered something Dad said about burning more fuel at top speed, but I couldn't bring myself to slow down. My jaw was clenched. It was all I could do not to reach behind and pick up the fuel tank and shake it to get a feel for just how much gas was left. But I didn't want to tilt it. I pictured the fuel hose inside the tank, slurping for fuel like a straw in a tilted cup.

It seemed a miracle that I made it to the mouth of Bluff Creek. But still, I was waiting for the motor to start coughing and sputtering at any moment.

Please, God, let me get home. Just this one time.

When I raced past Grover's dock I looked up at his house. I imagined him getting into his church clothes. I shut away the thought and faced the bayou again.

"Just this one time," I said aloud. And I knew there was something else I should add to my deal with God, but it would be another lie.

Once I was halfway up the bayou I started to feel I was actually going to make it. The waterway narrowed, and I raced between the trees. I had about a hundred yards to go when the motor started losing power. I reached behind and grabbed the fuel bulb and began squeezing it, sucking every drop of gas possible from the tank. The motor sped up and then slowed.

"Okay, God, I won't go out there again," I said. "Just let me get home and I won't go out there again."

The engine sputtered and died.

I took my hand off the throttle and looked at my dock a hundred yards away. I got out the paddle and began paddling the rest of the distance.

When I pulled up to the dock all was quiet. Normally

Dad would have already been walking out of the house to meet me. I tied the *Bream Chaser* to the dock and hurried inside. I saw Mom pass through the kitchen, brushing her hair. She stopped and looked at me.

"Sorry I'm late," I said. "I decided to come home and ride with you and Dad. Then I ran out of gas. I had to paddle a lot of the way."

"Ran out of gas?"

"Yes, ma'am. I guess I should have paid more attention to it."

Mom studied me. "Okay," she said. "Well, I'm glad it turned out all right. Hurry up and get showered and dressed. We're going to be late."

To my relief, Grover wasn't even at church that day. I remembered my plea to God and tried my best to pay attention to the sermon as repayment for any help He'd given me. The minister talked about a man in Jesus's time who was robbed on his way to Jericho. First a priest walked by without helping him. Then somebody called a Levite passed by and didn't help him either. Finally a Samaritan stopped and took care of the man and gave him a place to stay. And that's where they get the term "good Samaritan."

The whole point of the story was about being a good neighbor, and I couldn't help but think that I had acted like the good Samaritan with Davey. And maybe that canceled out the lies and deceit and danger.

But after church I just wanted the rest of the day to be normal. I didn't care about being a good Samaritan. When we got home I asked Dad to drive me to get more gas for the *Bream Chaser*. Along the way, he gave me a lecture about always checking the fuel level and I promised him that I would. When we got back to the house again I helped him hook his boat and trailer to the hitch on the car. We didn't load any fishing gear, but he said he just wanted to take her out and get the feel of things. It had been a while since he'd run the engine. We got Mom to ride with us to the public ramp so that she could drive back after we launched.

The only time I ever see Dad completely relaxed is when he's driving a boat. It's like the wind against his face blows away all of his thoughts of work and projects. Even if it weren't hard to talk over the noise of the outboard, I don't think he'd want to say much.

He drove us south, out the mouth of the Pascagoula River. The Mississippi Sound was calm that afternoon, with gentle swells clear out to the Gulf, where the water turned to a jade color and I could see the white-sand ripples of the bottom. Dad eventually slowed the boat and gazed out at the horizon.

"I know I've been working hard, Sam. And I'm sorry we haven't gotten to do more together so far this summer."

"It's all right," I said.

He turned to me. "No it's not. There's really no good excuse for it. For years I tried to get a promotion, and once I got it I was busy saving money for the house. Then I spent every weekend watching it get built. Now that all that's behind me, it seems I'm busier than ever at being a chief."

I didn't know what to say.

"Next weekend we're going fishing. Hell or high water."

I nodded. "Okay," I said.

He put his hand on my shoulder. "I couldn't ask for a better son. I should tell you that more often."

A little over a week ago I would have liked hearing those words and feeling his hand on my shoulder. Now it all made me feel terrible. I wasn't the boy he thought I was. The lies and deceit and shame burned inside me.

After supper that evening I settled into my beanbag chair to read some of a Gary Paulsen novel I'd been halfway through before all the stuff with my boat and Davey. Then I got into bed early and continued reading with the light of my bedside lamp. A few minutes later Mom came into my room and sat beside me on the bed. She looked deep into me and stroked my hair over my head with her fingers like I reminded her of somebody she was trying to remember. She used to straighten my hair all the time. I thought back to a few months before, when I was standing in the kitchen and her habit annoyed me. I'd pulled away and complained that I was too old for that. Now she didn't do it so much, and when she did it was just a quick brush like she couldn't help herself. And sometimes it was still annoying, but that night it felt good.

"Are you and Dad proud of me?"

Her look grew deeper and her eyes glistened in the weak light. "Of course we are, Sam. That's a silly question."

"Yeah," I said.

"Sam, you're doing everything right for a kid your age."

I wasn't, but it felt good to hear that she still thought so.

"There's nothing you can do to make us stop loving you," she said.

"Nothing?"

She patted my arm. "Nothing . . . Now, stop worrying and get some sleep," she said.

"Okay," I said.

She went out and pulled my door shut.

I put the book on my bedside table and turned off the lamp and lay there. I reminded myself not to think about Davey. Our time at the camp seemed so far away and long ago. But now, alone in the darkness, I couldn't keep my mind off the swamp. Slowly, it all crept into my head again and I was replaying everything I'd seen and heard and trying to put pieces together to make sense of it.

The missing dad, the money, the plan—Slade had mentioned something about a plan. What plan?

Something else wasn't sitting right with me. I remembered how Slade had seemed surprised to see Davey at the swamp camp. Like he never expected him to be there.

The unanswered questions built in my head. And I was certain Davey wasn't thinking about any of it nearly as much as he should. Right then he was probably lying on the hard floor of the camp, listening to his creepy brother and his friends talking in whispers and drinking beer and smoking cigarettes into the night, wondering when his father was going to show up.

Stop it, Sam. It's not your problem. They don't even want you around.

But I'd brought him food and helped him repair the camp and we'd become friends. I felt like I'd been kicked out of my own house and given no reason for it.

It's not your swamp camp, and it never was.

Then I thought about Grover calling Dad a redneck and Mom a crappy artist. After that, I didn't see how we could ever be friends again. It seemed everything was just getting worse when all I'd wanted was to make it better.

26

THE NEXT MORNING I SLEPT IN. THERE DIDN'T
seem to be any reason to get out of bed. About ten o'clock
Mom came into my room carrying the handset to the cord-
less phone.

"Sam, the Middletons' housekeeper called. She wanted to
know if Grover was here. She says she hasn't seen him since
early this morning. Have you heard from him at all?"

I sat up in bed and rubbed my eyes.

"No, ma'am," I said.

"He hasn't messaged you on the Xbox?"

I shook my head. "I haven't been playing it."

"She says his boat is gone."

"His boat?"

"That's right," she said.

"He doesn't even know how to drive it."

A concerned look came over Mom's face. She lifted the
handset and began dialing. "Let me call her back," she
said.

"Where's his dad?" I said.

Mom held up her hand for me to be quiet. I got out of bed and pulled on my shorts and slipped on a T-shirt.

"Hello, Natalia," Mom said over the phone. "Sam hasn't seen him . . . Okay . . . Okay . . . Yes, try to contact Dr. Middleton at the hospital, and I'll call Roger and get some help . . . I'm sure it will all be okay . . . Yes, I'll let you know."

Mom hung up the phone and looked at me. "Get your father's boat ready. I'll call and tell him to come home."

I untied the mooring lines on Dad's boat, walked it out of the slip, and secured it to the end of the dock. I was in the stern priming the fuel bulb when I saw him hurrying around the side of the house carrying his handheld radio.

Dad stepped into the boat without a word, took off his cap, and hung it on the throttle stick. Then he started the engine as I cast us off.

"So you don't know anything about this?" he said.

"No, sir," I said. "He's never even talked about his boat before."

"The housckeeper said he was upset about something last night. When she checked on him this morning he was gone."

"It doesn't make any sense that he would take the boat," I said.

"I called Jim Stockton. He's coming up from the south end of the river, and we should be able to search this end."

Dad shoved down on the throttle. The flats boat surged forward and leveled out, and we were soon racing down the bayou. I kept my eyes trained ahead of us, searching for any sign of Grover's Boston Whaler. It wasn't long before we passed his dock and I saw the cables to his lift dangling empty.

"He must have gone out on the river," I said back to Dad.

Dad nodded and swung the boat into Bluff Creek and pointed it toward the Pascagoula. When we got to the river he slowed the boat again and studied the waterway in both directions.

"I don't think he would have gone north," I said.

Dad frowned. "I hope not. If he did, it's not going to be easy to find him if he's lost."

Just then a voice came across Dad's radio.

"Roger, you read me?"

Dad unclipped the handheld from his waist and brought it to his mouth. "Yeah, Jim. Go ahead."

"I've been trying you for ten minutes," Officer Stockton said.

"Sorry. I've been running. Couldn't hear anything."

"Well, listen. I've got him. He's down here by the old lumberyard. He ran up into the dock."

"Is he okay?"

"Well, he's alive, but pretty banged up. A few broken bones, I imagine. There's an ambulance on the way."

"All right," Dad said. "We'll be there in a minute."

"Ten-four. See you shortly."

Dad clipped the radio back to his hip and gunned us down-river. In a few minutes we rounded a bend and I saw what must have been the abandoned lumberyard Officer Stockton was talking about. His patrol boat was tied to the river-bank with its blue lights strobing. Before it was Grover's Boston Whaler, smashed into a collapsed dock. The hull of the boat was cracked down the center, and the outboard motor was twisted and nearly torn off the stern.

"Good Lord," Dad said.

I didn't see Grover. As we drew closer I saw an ambulance parked behind a deserted warehouse, its red and white lights flashing and two medics carrying a stretcher toward it.

Dad cut the motor to an idle as we glided toward the patrol boat. Officer Stockton came out of the cabin, lowering his radio.

"Anything we can do?" Dad called out.

Officer Stockton shook his head. He gestured toward Grover's wrecked boat. "Lucky he's alive," he said.

I went to the bow and grabbed hold of the patrol boat as we came up next to it.

"What happened?" Dad asked.

Officer Stockton frowned. "Looks like he lost control. Wasn't even wearing a flotation vest."

"He's never driven it before," I said.

"Obviously," Officer Stockton said. "Fortunately, his dad's an orthopedic surgeon. He's going to meet the ambulance at the hospital."

Dad nodded and took a deep breath of relief through his nose. "Thanks, Jim," he said. "We'll check in on him later."

"Just glad he didn't kill himself," Officer Stockton said.

Dad backed the boat off and turned us toward home. He didn't speed up for a moment, and I figured he was trying to make sense of it all, just like me.

"How are things with Grover at home?"

"Fine, I guess."

Dad glanced at me.

"I mean, as far as I know," I said.

"His parents aren't around much, are they?"

"No, sir. Dr. Middleton works a lot, and Mrs. Middleton's always out of town."

"Who's usually there at the house with you guys?"

I sensed Dad was getting real close to discovering I hadn't been with Grover as much as I'd said I was.

"Their housekeeper, Natalia, most of the time," I said, "if his parents are gone."

"I don't like to get into other people's business, but that doesn't sound like much of a family."

I didn't respond. I just wanted to stop talking about it. To my relief, Dad pushed the throttle down and we sped back toward the house. It was too hard to talk over the engine noise.

As we rode along I couldn't help but think that Grover's accident had something to do with me. Something to do with the arguments we'd had and his strange behavior ever since. But I didn't know what him trying to drive his boat could have been meant to prove.

27

DAD WENT BACK TO THE OFFICE AFTER LUNCH and I got out the birdseed and walked about the yard loading Mom's three feeders. This wasn't something I usually did, but that day it was nice to have a mindless activity to smother my thoughts.

I heard Dad come in the front door about five o'clock as I was lying in bed catching up on my summer reading. A moment later he knocked on the bedroom door and I told him to come in.

"I talked to Dr. Middleton," he said from the doorway. "Grover's got a broken arm and two broken ribs, but he'll recover."

I set my book on the bedside table and sat up. "That's good," I said.

"Why don't you go over and check on him? He's back at his house now."

"It's kind of late," I said.

Dad glanced at the window. "You've got about three and a half hours of daylight left."

I didn't answer him.

"What's the problem?"

"I don't think Grover wants to see me," I said.

"Why not?"

I shook my head. "I don't really want to talk about it."

Dad hesitated, then came the rest of the way into my room and shut the door behind him. "Does this have anything to do with what happened today?"

"I don't know," I said. "Maybe."

He walked over and sat down on the bed beside me. He put his hand on my shoulder. "Son, tell me what's wrong."

I felt like I was about to cry, and the last thing I wanted to do was cry in front of him. I shook my head and swallowed against the words welling up inside me.

"I know something's been wrong," he said. "I should have asked you about it before now."

I shook my head again. I felt like if I said a single word I was going to lose control.

"I understand a man likes to work out his problems alone, but sometimes he needs some help."

I slid down onto the bed again and stared at the ceiling. I felt tears burning at the edges of my eyes. "It's just all messed up, Dad. Ever since the fight. I can't get it out of my head. I've just been doing stupid things trying to forget about it. I told Grover some mean things, and he said some mean things back, and now it's even more messed up than it ever was. I just wish it all hadn't happened."

"I told you that the fight didn't have anything to do with you. You *have* to believe that."

"But I *don't* believe it. I don't even want to talk to anybody at school, because I feel like they look at me and they can't stop thinking about it. Everybody saw it, Dad. Everybody. You think I don't think about girls? I used to all the time. Now all I think about is Julia's face watching me get beat up."

"Who's Julia?"

I shook my head at the thought.

"Just some girl," I said. "Like the prettiest girl in the class."

Dad breathed deep through his nose. "Those boys are criminals. They had no reason to do what they did, and everybody understands that. They're no different from muggers on the street. You think a mugger picks out who he's gonna rob?"

"He wouldn't pick *you*."

"No, probably not. I'm a cop."

"I know. And I'm nobody."

"Lord, you're a kid, Sam."

"Dad, they—Leroy and Gooch—waited for *us*. It was like they talked about it before we came out of the lunchroom."

I heard Dad take another deep breath.

"And I can't look at Grover without thinking about it. And I told him that, and I don't think we can ever be friends again."

"Sam, there's nothing wrong with you."

I wiped my face and nodded. "I just want to stop feeling like a loser."

"Let me tell you something. A loser is somebody who doesn't even try in life. That's not a word that should come into your head."

"I am trying, Dad. But I think I'm doing the wrong things."

"Like what?"

I couldn't tell him. I wanted to, but I couldn't. "I don't have any friends, Dad."

"We haven't even lived here a year. You're level-headed, trustworthy, honest, and loyal. You'll have no trouble making friends."

"Maybe I used to be all that."

"You're just a little confused right now. Grover's not your problem. And you can go over to his house right now and get everything back on track."

"I want to stop thinking about the fight. I just want it to go away."

"It will. It may take some time, but it will. You and Grover probably should have talked about it a while back."

I nodded.

"He might need you more than ever now. Just because a person won't ask for help doesn't mean you shouldn't give it to him. Being a man isn't about winning fights and carrying guns. It's about helping people however you can, no matter what. That's why I do what I do. And I can tell you, I didn't figure it out until I was much older than you."

"Okay," I said. And somehow I felt like I'd been forgiven of a lot of things, even the things I hadn't told him about.

"Sit up," he said.

I sat up and rubbed at my eyes again with my shirtsleeve.

Dad patted me on the back. "Life's hard sometimes. You can't always figure it all out by yourself. That's why I married your mother."

I smiled.

"Feeling better?"

"A little. I really don't want to go over there. But I guess I have to."

"No, you don't have to—and I won't make you. But my guess is that you will, because you know it's the right thing to do."

I wasn't sure I believed what Dad was telling me, but I didn't even believe myself anymore.

28

GOING TO SEE GROVER SOUNDED EASY WHEN I was talking to Dad about it. Once I was in my boat headed for his house, though, I got a sick feeling like I was about to walk into a party where I wasn't welcome. But I told myself that it was something I had to get through no matter how it came out. And then I would have at least tried, and there was nothing more to be done after that.

I entered through the empty sitting room as I normally did, thinking maybe Grover had moved back into his lair. But when I walked into the basement it was still neat and tidy like he hadn't been there. I started up the stairs and suddenly felt like a stranger in his house. I stopped and listened.

"Hello?" I called.

I heard footsteps approaching, and in a moment Natalia was looking down the staircase at me.

"Hi, Sam," she said. "Grover's up here in his room."

"Is it okay if I visit him?"

I wanted her to say no. I wanted more than anything to put all this off for later.

"Of course it is," she said. "I think he'd really appreciate it."

I started up again. "Thanks," I said.

When I got to the top of the stairs she stepped aside for me
to pass. Then she reached out and grabbed my arm.

"Sam," she said.

I turned back to her. She studied me like she was trying to
read my mind.

"He's having a hard time," she said.

"I know," I said.

"I'm worried about him."

"I'm just here to be his friend," I said.

She let go of my arm and smiled sadly. "Good," she said.
"He needs that right now."

I continued down the hall and knocked on Grover's door.
He didn't answer, so I pushed it open and saw him sitting up
in bed watching me. His right arm lay in his lap, sealed up to
his shoulder in a cast. He had his shirt off and his torso was
wrapped in gauze. His face was bandaged in several places.

"Man," I said. "Does it hurt pretty bad?"

"Yeah," he said dryly. "It hurts pretty bad."

I walked over to a chair beside his bed and sat down.
Grover's eyes followed and stayed on me.

"Guess I can't do anything right," he said.

"Why didn't you just ask me to show you how to drive
your boat?"

"Maybe because you said you didn't ever want to see me again."

I looked at the floor. "I shouldn't have said that."

"Well, you did."

"Yeah, I know."

"You think I don't know how you feel about the fight? You think I'm that dense?"

I looked up at him. "You never talked about it."

"Neither did you. Maybe I'm embarrassed, too. Maybe I'm a lot more embarrassed than you, because everything you said is true. I got nothing going for me, Sam. And the last thing I want is to think about that too much."

"You've got everything, Grover. You've got more stuff than anybody I know."

"Yeah, and I don't know how to use any of it except the Xbox. And even if I did, what fun would it be? Nobody cares what I do. How much fun do you think it is getting to level seven in Demon Quest when nobody's there to see it? How much fun is it to catch a fish when your mom's not around to cook it and your dad doesn't give a crap about it?"

"It's not that bad, Grover."

"Really? Where's my dad now? I almost die in a boat wreck, and he sends another doctor in to fix me up and calls Natalia to bring me home because he's still working."

"He probably just can't leave. He's probably got operations to do."

"Mom's in Belize. She probably doesn't even know. I don't even know when she's coming home. I don't even know why they're still married."

I didn't know what to say.

"Actually," Grover continued, "I know why they're still married. I heard them yelling at each other a few months ago, and he told her the only reason he didn't divorce her was because it would cost too much."

"You never told me any of that, Grover."

"Of course I didn't. You were the only shot I had at a friend, and I didn't want to ruin it. I couldn't tell you anything."

"I'm still your friend," I said.

"But you've got new friends now. I'm sure they're a lot more fun. And they probably know how to do more than play video games."

"I didn't think you'd take your boat out by yourself."

"Yeah, I'm scared to death of it. I hardly even know how to swim. You think I want anybody to know that?"

"I'm a good driver," I said. "We can take my boat. We'll be fine."

"Well, why'd you start all this? You really think I can just change all of a sudden? Learn all this stuff?"

"It's the fight, Grover. Ever since the fight I've been messed up in the head. I thought I wanted to change myself. I thought I had to go off and do my own thing and that you wouldn't understand."

"Well, no, I wouldn't understand, not when you don't tell me anything."

"So I went looking for that dead guy they were talking about on the news. I thought if I did something really scary and brave it would help. And then I met this kid named Davey in the swamp. He was living out there by himself. I started taking things to him and helping him. And it felt good to hang out with somebody who didn't know about what happened."

"*That's* who needed your help? How is there a kid living in the swamp?"

"There used to be camps out there, you know? And this camp used to be his family's a long time ago, and he went out there this summer and started fixing it up. He told me his brother and his dad were coming, but they never did. And this past weekend I told my parents that I was spending the night with you, and I went out there and stayed with him. And then his brother finally showed up with some friends, and I think they're all a bunch of outlaws. I think it's their hideout."

Grover stared at me. "That's the craziest thing I've ever heard. Nobody has hideouts anymore. That's like from old movies. Like fifty years ago."

"Davey's got all this money, Grover. Like thousands of dollars. He said his brother gave it to him. And he just wants a family so bad that he doesn't even ask where it came from.

He doesn't even want it. He tried to give it to me. But I know they stole it. Officer Stockton, the same guy who found you today, came to our house and told us about a fish market that got robbed and described a boat that looks just like theirs."

"So let me get this straight. You have a new friend who's a homeless thief? And being friends with him is an upgrade from me?"

"Davey's not a thief, Grover. His brother is. Davey's in big trouble, and he won't admit it."

"Well, where's their dad? Is he a thief, too?"

"I don't know. He still hadn't gotten there by the time I left. Davey said he's not a thief, but there's a lot of it that doesn't add up. Anyway, Davey doesn't care. He won't give up hope that they can be some kind of normal family again."

Grover reached over to his bedside table and grabbed a glass of water. He took a sip and set it down. "I don't know much about normal families," he said, "but I don't think there's any chance of *them* being normal."

"I just left him out there, Grover. I feel really bad about it."

"You've been leaving a lot of people lately."

"I know. I feel bad about everything."

"I can't believe I talked Natalia into taking me to church last Sunday. What a waste." Grover looked out the window for a moment.

"I'm sorry," I said.

He frowned. "I didn't mean what I said about your dad. Or your mom."

"I know. You were just upset."

"Your dad is five times the man my dad is. And I'd give anything to have your mother. Natalia's more like a mom to me than anybody. But nobody needs a mom they order around and call by their first name."

"I've never heard you order her around."

"Well, I could . . ."

I didn't mean to smile, but it just came out as relief washed over me that Grover was no longer upset with me.

"So what are you going to do about Davey?" he said.

"I don't know. Dad said sometimes you have to try and help people even when you think they don't want it."

"I don't imagine your dad knows about your outlaw friend in the swamp?"

"Funny."

"Why don't you tell him? Get Davey's brother and friends arrested. Get your dad to handle it."

"Davey says they'll send him back to a foster home. He says he'll drown himself before he lets that happen. He told me how he got treated at the last one, and I don't blame him for thinking that way."

"So you just have to go talk him into it."

"I've tried."

"I didn't think you were ever going to talk to me again,

Sam. If you hadn't come over here today, I might have done something else stupid."

"What do you mean?"

"I mean just what your dad said: sometimes you think a person doesn't want your help, but they do."

29

I LEFT GROVER'S HOUSE FEELING LIGHTER, THE weight of our arguments finally off me. Although my stomach was heavy, because Natalia had fixed us some big sandwiches for supper.

I slept well for the first time in many nights. When I got up, Dad was gone but Mom was still at the house. She said she was going in to work a little late and wanted to have breakfast with me. She scrambled some eggs and brought them to the dining room table and set them before me with a glass of milk. Then she went back into the kitchen and returned with a cup of coffee and sat in the chair across from me and watched me eat. It didn't bother me. I was used to her doing that. Like she was remembering things and maybe a little sad for some reason.

"How are things with Grover?" she asked.

"He's got a cast on and a lot of bandages, but he seems to be doing okay."

"I mean with you and Grover."

"Dad told you?"

Mom nodded.

"It's okay now," I said.

"You two have been through a lot together. Whether you realize it or not, he's always going to be a close friend."

"I know," I said.

"You don't always get to pick your friends, you know. Sometimes they pick you. And those are the best kind."

"Sometimes he's just so annoying."

"I've never had a friend who wasn't just a little bit annoying in some way."

"He can be *real* annoying in *lots* of ways."

Mom smiled like she understood. "Grover's got a lot of character," she said. "That's what makes him interesting."

"Yeah," I said. And everything about Grover suddenly made sense. "It's like he's so boring that he's not boring," I said.

Mom raised her eyebrows and nodded like she hadn't thought of it that way.

"But we're fine," I said. "It's all fine."

Mom seemed relieved, and I saw that the hint of sadness in her eyes was gone.

"Anything else you want to talk to me about?" she asked.

I took a drink of milk and shook my head slowly like I couldn't think of anything. Then I did think of something I'd been wanting to ask. And I thought it was the perfect time to steer the conversation in another direction.

"Actually," I said, "I do have one thing."

"Okay," she said.

"You told me once that our church helps people find foster homes."

Mom looked a little surprised. "Yes," she said. "I've actually been part of that process. They place several children a year with new families."

"Does it usually work? I mean, are the kids happy?"

"There's always exceptions, but I think they've been successful. According to the files I've seen, most of the kids have ended up being adopted, and a lot of them have gone on to college and done just fine for themselves."

"What if a kid didn't like his new family?"

Mom eyed me suspiciously. "What's with the sudden interest in foster homes?"

"I'm just curious," I said. "You never talk much about what you do."

"Well, I typically just help with the paperwork. There's a volunteer group that does most of the placement."

"So you would know if it didn't work?"

"It works. They spend a lot of time interviewing the families and making sure they think it's a good match for both the child and the parents."

"Do they go and check on them to see if they're okay?"

"Sometimes. The state is also supposed to check on them."

"Has the church ever found out the parents were being mean?"

"Like abuse? No, never anything like that. All of the families we've worked with have been good people."

"But how would you know?"

"If you've done it as long as we have, you get a certain feeling about things. We can generally tell who's fit to be a foster parent and who's not."

I nodded to myself.

"Anything else?" she asked.

I shook my head.

She brushed her hair behind her ear and stood.

"I better get to work," she said.

"All right," I said. "Dad wants me to mow the lawn, and then I might take the boat out."

"Okay. Wear your flotation vest and be safe."

Later, I got the lawn mower out of the shed, gassed it, checked the oil, and generally took my time checking it over. Then I pull-started it and began pushing it over the lawn in a slow, deliberate pattern. I felt good to be doing something I knew was right and responsible. It felt good to put off my return to the swamp for a few more hours and lose my thoughts behind the steady engine noise. I really didn't want to think any more about it. I really didn't want to go.

Although it had only been a couple of days since I'd been there, the swamp seemed like a different place. I was no longer

scared of the black water and the looming trees and the isola-
tion and the quiet. I felt like an expert now. Like there was
no way I couldn't get in and out without trouble.

When I finally slowed at the mouth of Ware Bayou cicadas were starting to buzz in the trees as late-afternoon summer heat settled over me. Even though I was still several bends
away from Davey's camp, I listened anyway, half expecting
to hear him and the others across the miles of emptiness. I
heard nothing but the insects and the reeds swishing to the
disturbance of my boat wake. I motored slowly around the
deadhead and continued on.

When I came around the last bend I saw no one on the
deck. Slade's boat was tied up, but Davey's canoe was gone
and the catfish jugs had been left untended and were tangled
in the weeds. I shut off my motor and drifted to the dock. I
looked and listened. There was loose trash lying about, and
the grill was out like someone had been there recently. But I
heard nothing.

"Hello?" I said quietly as I got out of the boat and went up
to the camp.

No one answered. The confidence I'd been feeling on the
trip out was quickly ebbing away. There was something eerie
about being here at the camp. It was no longer Davey's play-
house. It was something more serious now. Something sinister
and uninviting.

I walked onto the deck of the camp. It didn't seem like

they'd made any repairs since I'd left. The front door was still missing, and there was a pile of loose nails at my feet. I continued inside and saw blankets and sleeping bags piled on the floor and hanging sloppily from the bunk. I saw Baldy's pot on the kitchen counter next to some fly-covered McDonald's trash, empty beer cartons, and a half-empty two-liter bottle of Coke.

I walked back out onto the deck and looked down to where Davey's canoe had been. The marsh grass was still flattened and the drag marks were fresh. It wasn't possible that all four of them had left in Davey's canoe. It didn't make sense that the camp was abandoned with Slade's boat still there.

Unless someone had come and gotten them.

My eyes wandered up and studied the trail leading into the trees. There were fresh footprints in the mud.

"Davey?" I said. But I didn't say it loud enough for anyone to hear. I don't think I wanted anyone to hear. I certainly didn't want to go up that trail. Somehow I knew that whatever was back there wasn't something I wanted to see. I'd known this since the first time Davey had pointed it out and acted like he didn't know what it was.

I dropped down into the marsh grass and walked over to the muddy footpath. The buzz of cicadas was suddenly louder as I approached the gap in the vines and palmettos that created something like a cave entrance into the depths of the swamp. Mosquitoes hung in the air and whined about my face. Beyond, there was only darkness and shadow and the rich smell of rotten vegetation.

I swept the vines from my face and pushed through the palmettos and stepped into the damp, shadowy bottomland. The swamp was more open than I'd imagined beyond the wall of thicket lining the creek bank. The canopy rose far overhead and closed above me. I only saw the sunlight in dappled patches, far up in the tops of the trees and sometimes falling on a single palmetto frond near my hand. I heard strange birdcalls that I hadn't noticed before, shrill and distant. I looked at my feet and saw the footprints beckoning me into the dim light.

I pushed on slowly, waving the mosquitoes from my face, my ears trained on every sound, but only hearing the faraway birdcalls. Always in the distance like they were constantly moving away from me. I kept going until finally I heard the birds behind me. I stopped and turned in a circle, and everything looked the same. If I hadn't had the trail, I knew I'd be lost. And suddenly the fear that I'd lose the trail gripped me, and I studied my own footprints until the fear subsided. Then I was left with my heavy breathing and an instant thirst and was wishing I'd thought to bring water. I slapped a mosquito on my cheek. The birdcalls came to my ears again. And something else this time. I thought I heard voices.

"Davey?" I said. The sound of my own voice frightened me, and I was glad I hadn't spoken loud enough for anyone to hear. If I'd really heard voices at all. If I hadn't imagined it.

I took a deep breath and continued up the trail, wishing the raspy palmettos brushing across my waist weren't so loud.

Wishing I could hear better. Then I *did* hear something. Someone let out a shout in the distance, and I stopped and stared in the direction it came from. I trained my eyes on the weave of vines and fronds, studying the patterns they made against the tree trunks. Slowly I looked off-trail to my left. My eyes passed, then jerked back to something that seemed out of place. My heart leaped in my chest when I saw the doll face staring back at me. Slade standing still as a statue, partially camouflaged against the backdrop of the swamp.

30

IT SEEMED THAT SLADE STUDIED ME FOR A FULL minute, as if he wasn't sure I saw him. And then he said, "Kid," and the sound of his voice came to me like he was closer than he looked.

"Where's Davey?" I said.

He began walking, pressing through the palmettos. When he reached the trail in front of me he turned on it and came toward me until he was standing over me. His doll face was slick and sweaty, and his hands were dirty like he'd been digging in the mud.

"He's not here," Slade said in a way that scared me. In a way that told me I wasn't welcome.

"Where is he?" I asked.

"I don't know," he said, like he was saying one thing but thinking another.

"I just—"

"You just couldn't leave it alone, could you?"

"I don't know what you mean."

"Didn't you get the idea we don't want you around?"

I didn't know how to answer him. "I just wanted to talk to Davey," I said.

"Why don't you talk to me? What is it you need to tell him so bad?"

"I don't know," I said.

"Slade!" someone shouted.

I looked past him and saw Fred coming down the trail.

"What are you doin'?" Fred said.

"Come here, Fred," Slade said without taking his eyes off me.

Then Fred came closer and saw me. "What's he doin' here?"

"He came to help us," Slade said.

Fred stopped beside him and looked at me. "What?"

"Yeah," Slade continued. "Let's show him what we need him to do."

Fred looked at him in disbelief. "Are you kiddin' me?"

Slade turned to him. "No," he said. "He just got himself a job. And solved one of our problems."

There was nowhere to run, no one to call for help. I had no choice but to follow Fred with Slade right behind me. We continued down the trail until we came to a small open area where there was more sunlight. At the other side of the clearing Jesse was sitting on a log drinking from a jug of water. It made me feel better to see him. I had gotten the sense that he was the only one of them who might protect Davey—and me—from Slade. When he saw me he lowered the jug and a worried look came over him.

"What are you doin' with *him*?" Jesse said.

"He came lookin' for Davey," Fred replied.

Jesse shook his head. "So you couldn't just take him back to the camp?"

"I've got an idea," Slade said. "We need him."

Jesse set down the jug and stood and used the back of his arm to wipe sweat from his forehead. "There's no way this can be good, Slade," he said.

"I'm not askin' for your opinion," Slade said.

Jesse frowned and kept his eyes on Fred until Fred looked away.

Slade pointed at the ground. "You know what that is, kid?"

I studied it. At first I didn't notice anything special about it except for the sunlight falling across the tops of the plants. Then I noticed that the plants were different from any others I'd passed. They were tall and leafy.

"No," I said.

"That's marijuana."

I stared at it and swallowed. "You mean, like the drug?" I said.

Slade chuckled. "Yeah, like the drug."

I looked at Jesse. He had his jaw clenched, staring off into the trees like he was trying to keep from saying anything.

"I don't know anything about that," I said, hearing my voice crack.

"Well, you do now," Jesse said, stomping past us and back down the trail.

"Hey—" Fred started to say something to Jesse.

"Let him go," Slade interrupted.

"I just want to talk to Davey for a little while and then go home," I said.

"That's fine," Slade said. "We're gonna let you go home. But you're gonna take some of this with you. And you're gonna take it to a friend of mine."

"I don't want to," I said.

Suddenly Slade grabbed me by the shirt and pulled me close to him. I saw the sweat beads rolling down his face. I smelled the sour beer and cigarette stench of his breath. "I'm not askin' you what you want," he hissed. "Playtime's over. You got yourself into this, and now you're a part of it. And if you screw it up, I'm gonna come to your house on Acorn Drive and kill you in your sleep."

My mind raced with fear at the thought of Slade creeping through my house at night and standing over me with a knife. And I had no doubt that he'd do it. Leroy Parnell and Gooch were nothing compared to this guy. They were just dumb kids. Slade was the real deal.

I had no choice but to follow them back up the trail to the camp. They weren't turning to check on me, and I thought about running, but we all knew there was nowhere for me to go. And Slade's threat had me paralyzed with fear.

"Where you think Jesse ran off to?" Fred said.

"He better get his attitude straight," Slade grumbled.

"I'm hungry, anyway," Fred replied.

"Jesse better not set foot in that boat," Slade said. "I'll kill him and his dog."

As we walked I didn't notice the bird sounds or the cicadas or the mosquitoes. I watched my feet moving up the trail while my ears hummed with fear and my mind raced with escape plans. But I couldn't think of any way out of the situation. The whole thing seemed like a bad dream that I'd wake up from.

Why did I come back? Everything was fine. Why did I do this?

When we broke from the swamp I saw the creek again and Davey's canoe pulled onto the bank in its usual spot. Then I saw Davey standing on the deck looking out at me, and I breathed a sigh of relief.

I climbed after the older boys up onto the deck. Slade stepped down onto the dock, got into the *Bream Chaser*, disconnected the fuel hose, and tied it around his waist like a loose belt. He walked past me and Davey and went into the camp with Fred following. Then I heard Fred inside arguing with Jesse in low voices about something I couldn't make out.

I turned and faced Davey. He was staring at me like he'd been watching me the whole time.

"You shouldn't have come back," he said to me, like we'd never been friends at all.

"I didn't know," I said.

He kept staring at me.

"I wanted to talk to you," I said.

Davey looked at the camp. "Slade," he called.

"Yeah?" Slade replied irritably.

"I need to tell you somethin'."

"Then tell me."

"Come out here."

"I can hear you. Tell me."

Davey hesitated. "His dad's a cop."

31

MY HEART BEGAN TO BEAT HEAVILY AT DAVEY'S words. I felt heat rush to my face.

Slade stepped out of the camp. He stared at Davey. "What?"

Davey wouldn't look at me. "His dad's a cop," he repeated.

Jesse appeared behind Slade in the doorway. "I'm done with all this," he said.

Slade spun and shoved him against the door frame, shaking the whole camp. "You're not done with anything, Jesse!"

Then Slade glanced at me before turning back to Davey. I saw anger building in his eyes.

"How long have you known this?"

"The whole time," Davey replied with a shaky voice.

"Why didn't you say anything?"

"I . . . I didn't think it mattered. Not at first."

"Davey didn't know we were growin' pot out there," Jesse said. "He didn't know anything."

Slade kept his eyes on Davey. "Well, he's known for two days now!" he shouted at him.

Davey sank to the deck and hugged his knees to his chest like I'd seen him do the day after the storm.

"My God, don't start that again," Slade said.

"This whole plan of yours is off the rails!" Jesse shouted.

Slade turned and grabbed him by the throat with one hand. Jesse swung and hit him in the stomach. This only enraged Slade more. He grabbed Jesse's shirt with both hands, dragged him to the center of the deck, stepped back, and punched him in the face. Jesse staggered and fell. He took a moment to shake it off, then pushed himself up into a sitting position.

"This has been a screw-up since day one!" Jesse shouted. "You're gonna get us all arrested!"

Fred appeared in the doorway with a confused look.

Jesse started to stand, but Slade kicked him hard in the ribs and he went down again, clutching his side.

"Come on, Slade," Fred urged.

Slade spun and looked at him. "You want some of this, Fred?"

"No, it's just—"

"Shut up, then!"

"Just let the kid go, man."

Slade turned and kicked Jesse again as he was getting to his knees. Jesse went down on his stomach and moaned. Slade watched him, fury boiling in his head. I looked at Davey. He was still balled up, and now he had his hands over his ears.

"Ain't nobody goin' anywhere," Slade said, still staring at Jesse.

"Well, what are we gonna do about the kid?" Fred said.

Slade turned to him. "We're gonna do just what we talked about. We're gonna bag a few plants and he's gonna take it to Walter in his cute little dinghy. And if he screws up, I'm gonna come to his house in the middle of the night and cut his throat."

"His dad's a cop, Slade!" Fred shouted.

Slade looked at me. "I don't care what he is. We're gonna be out of here by the time the kid makes the delivery."

"I don't think it's a good idea. Why can't *we* just do it?" Fred said.

Slade shook his head and looked down at Jesse like he wanted to kick him again. But Jesse was lying still on his side, holding his ribs and staring off over the creek. Slade shook his head and spit on him. Then he looked at their boat.

"What about Daddy?" Davey said.

Slade didn't answer him.

"I just can't get to the end of how stupid you people are," Slade said. "We got a big grow to haul in and deliver. With a stolen boat. If we get pulled over, we're screwed. They won't think twice about the kid here."

Fred thought about it for a few seconds and finally nodded.

Slade turned to him. "So you got that in your thick skull?"

"Yeah," Fred said. "I guess you got a point."

Slade looked down at Jesse again. "How about you, Jesse? You think you get it now?"

Jesse didn't answer.

"Well, it don't matter if you get it or not. That's how it's gonna be . . . Nobody leaves until they've done their job and I say it's time to go."

"But what about Daddy?" Davey said again.

Slade spun and looked at him. "Will you shut up about that? He's not comin'! You know he's not comin', so stop askin' me about it."

Davey stared at him with a blank expression.

"Surely you're not that stupid," Slade said.

"What do you mean, he's not comin'?"

"I don't even know where he is," Slade said.

"How can you not know where he is, Slade?"

"Why would it matter? He never cared about either one of us."

"That's not true," Davey said.

"Yeah, well, why isn't he out here? I thought you'd be gone by the time I got back here. I told him where you were, and he didn't come get you. So there you have it."

"You told him I was out here?"

"That's what I said."

Davey started to say something, but didn't. He sat against the outside wall and hugged his knees to his chest and stared over the creek.

Slade turned and started into the camp. "And don't start your baby act about it," he said over his shoulder.

Fred followed Slade into the camp, and Jesse propped

himself up and scooted over and sat against the wall next to Davey.

"Don't listen to him," Jesse said.

Davey didn't respond.

The three of us sat there as darkness settled over the swamp, none of us talking, each of us trying to figure a way out of our problems. We strained to hear Slade and Fred inside, discussing their plans, but we couldn't make out the details. After an hour they came back outside. Fred carried two flashlights, and Slade was no longer wearing the fuel hose around his waist.

Slade stood over Jesse. "You might as well stay here. Fred and I just voted you out."

Jesse looked up at him. "Fine. But I want my share of the fish market money."

"Tough crap," Fred said.

Jesse looked away and shook his head. Slade stood over him a moment longer, then went to their boat, took the fuel hose from it, and tied it around his waist where the other had been. "Just in case any of you get any ideas," he said.

Slade came back onto the deck and looked down at Davey. "What about you? You with us or them?"

Davey looked up. "I'm with you, Slade. I'm always with you."

"Well, I'm not so sure."

"Don't say that, Slade," Davey pleaded.

"You just remember who's family and who's not."

"I do," Davey insisted. "I always do."

Slade stared at him for a few seconds. "Good. You stay here, then," he said. "Keep an eye on these two. Come get me if anybody tries to leave."

Davey looked at the deck and nodded.

"Look at me and say okay," Slade said.

Davey looked up at him again. "Okay," he said.

32

AS SOON AS SLADE AND FRED DISAPPEARED UP the trail into the swamp Jesse stood up.

"Hell with him," he said.

He went inside, where I heard him scraping about in the kitchen.

"You want something to eat?" Davey said softly.

I shook my head.

"I had to tell him," Davey said.

I didn't answer.

"I thought if I told him your dad was a cop, then he wouldn't make you deliver the drugs."

I looked at him. "I don't trust you anymore," I said.

Davey swallowed, and I could see that my words hurt him.

"I don't want anybody to go to jail," he said.

"I don't think your brother cares what you want."

Davey looked at his knees again and didn't respond.

Jesse appeared, stuffing the last bite of a sandwich in his mouth. He leaned against the doorjamb.

"Your dad got out earlier or somethin'. He wasn't at the prison when Slade went to pick him up."

"But where is he?" Davey asked.

"I don't know."

"Why'd Slade say he was comin'?"

"At first Slade just lied to you so you'd stop buggin' him about it. He didn't know where your dad was."

"Why'd he send me out here?"

"He didn't know what else to do with you. He got kicked out of his house a month ago. He's got nowhere to live. He can't haul you around and let you sleep on his friends' couches. Then your dad caught up with Slade and found out he'd sent you here. From what I heard, your dad was pretty upset about it and was supposed to come get you."

"But he never did."

"I guess not," Jesse said.

I turned back to Davey. "One of my dad's friends is a marine policeman. He's looking for Slade, and he knows y'all are out here somewhere."

Jesse shook his head.

"That's why I came out here again," I continued. "To tell you that. And to say you had to come back with me."

"Slade knows what to do," Davey said.

"Slade doesn't know crap," Jesse said. "Slade's out of control. And as soon as we leave here, he'll dump you off somewhere else."

"Where's the fuel hose to my boat?" I said. "We three can leave right now."

Davey pulled his knees up again and began shaking his head.

"Where'd he put it, Davey?" Jesse said.

Davey didn't budge.

Jesse went into the camp and I heard him tossing things around. Davey rested his chin on his knees and stared over the creek. Tears welled in his eyes like he couldn't keep his thoughts from pushing them out.

After a few minutes Jesse returned. "I can't find it. But I didn't see him take it with him."

"Come on, Davey," I said. "Where is it?"

"Slade's all I've got left," he mumbled. Tears began rolling down his face. He looked at me. "What if I make him mad, Sam? What if I make him mad and he doesn't want me to live with him?"

I watched Davey.

"Did you hear what I said a minute ago?" Jesse said. "Slade doesn't have anywhere to live. And even if he did have somewhere to take you, it wouldn't last. He wouldn't stick it out for long."

Davey wiped the tears from his face. "I'm not goin' back to a foster home," he said stubbornly.

"My mom told me there's good ones. She knows that because of where she works," I said. "And I can come see you. And maybe we'll be in the same school."

Davey stared over the creek again. After a moment he got

up and went into the camp. He came back with the fuel hose and dropped it before me.

I grabbed the hose and stood.

"Let me get my things," Jesse said.

I nodded and turned to Davey. "Thanks."

Davey didn't answer me.

Jesse returned with a backpack over his shoulder and went down to the *Bream Chaser*.

"Get in the boat, Davey," I said.

"You left your other friend because he embarrassed you," Davey said.

"I was wrong. I told him I was sorry."

"But that's how you felt."

"I was confused, Davey."

"Slade's all I've got."

"You have to come with me, Davey."

He looked at me for a moment. Then he pulled a small flashlight from his pocket and turned and dropped down into the marsh. He took a few steps up the trail before turning back again. "You better get goin'," he said.

33

DAVEY WAS GONE INTO THE SWAMP BEFORE I HAD a chance to argue with him. I figured whatever time he could give us before he alerted Slade to our escape might not be enough. I had a long way to go and a slower boat.

"Let's get out of here," Jesse said. "There's nothin' more we can do for him."

I hesitated, but I knew he was right. Jesse got onto the front seat and untied us while I started the motor. He shoved us off and I gunned the boat up the dark creek, keeping my navigation lights off, running blind and shooting the gap between the cut in the swamp canopy. The way the tops of the trees patterned against the sky glow was enough to give me a rough estimation of where the middle of the creek was. I thought about Davey, somewhere out there on the trail, with his tiny flashlight, walking toward a horrible fate. It was like he'd died.

I stared straight ahead into the faint path of this canyon between the trees. I was going home for good now. Leaving all this behind. Finally, there was nothing left for me to do.

This swamp camp would always be a dark secret—as if I'd really found the dead body and I could never tell about it.

But the swamp, suddenly evil and menacing again, wasn't about to let me go so easily. The boat slammed into something and I was thrown forward. I crashed into the front seat and heard the motor screaming at the night. Then it made a clattering sound and died. After a moment I came to my senses and pushed myself up and pieced it all together. I'd hit the deadhead. Like it had been lying in wait for me all these days. Put there especially for me.

Jesse wasn't in the boat. Then I heard something splashing around in the darkness and saw the dark form of a person in the water near the creek bank.

I crawled to the back of the boat and looked at the motor. It was tilted up at a strange angle, silent and dripping. I looked for Jesse again. I saw him crawling into the marsh.

"You all right?" he said to me.

"Yeah," I said.

"What happened?"

"We hit a log."

"Is my backpack still in there?"

I thought it was a strange question. I scanned the front of the boat and saw it lying under the seat.

"Yeah," I said. "It's under the front seat."

"Good. Get the boat started again and come get me. Hurry."

I reached around behind the motor for the tilt mechanism. My hands shook so much it was hard to grasp it. I finally got hold and lowered the foot of it back into the water. I started the engine and put it into gear. The boat didn't move. I raced the motor just to be sure, but I already knew what was wrong.

"I sheared the pin," I said.

"What does that mean?"

"The prop won't turn until I fix it."

"How long's that gonna take? We've got to get out of here quick."

I turned off the motor, slipped over the side of the boat into the creek, and began swimming it toward Jesse. "I don't know," I said. "I need you to help me."

"I don't know anything about it."

"I think I can do it," I said. "I just can't do it by myself."

I felt mud underfoot and pressed my feet into it and shoved the boat forward. I sloshed into the marsh and came around the side of the boat and pulled it into the reeds. Then I tipped the engine out of the water.

"What do I do?" Jesse said.

"There's a cotter pin holding the prop nut on. Use these to take it off." I gave him a pair of pliers from the emergency kit that was stowed in a well at the bow of the boat.

Jesse waded back to the motor and began working on the prop. I climbed into the boat and pulled off the engine cowling and got the spare pin. I stuck it in my mouth and replaced the cowling. Jesse got the prop off and held it up like he didn't know what to do with it. I told him to put the nut and cotter pin into his front pocket. I took the prop from him, set it on the deck of the boat, and slipped into the water again.

"I've got to get—"

We both heard Slade's engine crank at the same time, the noise of it traveling all the way down the creek through the quiet night.

"We don't have time for this," Jesse said. He waded alongside the boat and got his backpack from under the seat. Then he tossed it up into the trees.

I listened to the sound of Slade's motor accelerate and race toward us.

"Come on!" Jesse said. "We've got to get out of here."

He crashed through the grass and into the underbrush. My mind raced as I tried to decide what to do. I took the shear pin out of my mouth and shoved it into my pocket. Then I rushed to the bow and reached in and got a flare from the emergency box. I shoved it into my pocket and hurried after Jesse.

After fighting a wall of briars and vines and palmettos, I broke through into the dark cavern of the interior swamp.

"Over here," I heard Jesse say.

I followed the sound of his voice, stepping slowly and waving my hands before my face to feel for trees and clear any spiderwebs and vines. Slade's boat seemed like it was almost upon us.

"Where are you?" I said.

"Over here," Jesse said. "I found an animal trail. Hurry."

I kept going, my eyes adjusting to the darkness until I could make out the silhouette of him standing a few feet away to my left. As I approached he turned and pulled me ahead of him. "Hurry," he said. "Stay in front of me."

I kept on, occasionally tripping over a tree root or sloshing through a small stream. The trail was definitely made by things shorter than us, as there were still spiderwebs and branches at chest level. But the ground was free of obstructions and there was a gap in the palmettos. I moved as fast as possible with the sound of Slade's boat remaining clear, like we weren't making much progress at all.

I began to smell something dead. The swamp was always so full of wet, fetid smells that I didn't think much of it. Then I tripped and fell over a large, soft obstacle in the path. I knew right away that it was a dead animal of some sort. I had kicked away from it and started to crawl when Jesse tumbled over me. Then both of us were untangling ourselves and scrambling forward.

"What the hell was that?" he said.

We heard Slade's engine slow and the boat waves crash against the creek bank.

"It's something dead," I whispered.

I heard Jesse crawl off the trail into the palmettos.

"Get away from it," he said. "Come over here and be still."

I followed and backed into a tree next to him.

"Be still," he said again.

I stopped moving until all I heard was the sound of Jesse breathing and the boat motor that seemed like it wasn't more than a hundred feet from us.

"Look," I heard Fred say.

"I see it," Slade replied. "Check out the motor. The prop's gone."

I heard his outboard engine shut off and Jesse's breathing grow heavier.

"You goin' after them?" Fred said.

"They're not far," Slade replied.

I saw a spotlight beam pass through the trees overhead.

"You messed up, Jesse!" Slade yelled. "You might as well come out of there and give me back the money!"

I looked at Jesse. I saw the backpack hugged into his lap. Then I felt his hand go over my mouth and press me hard against the tree. I sat there, breathing through my nose, pulling in the heavy stench of the dead thing, listening to mosquitoes whine about my face.

"Jesse!" Slade yelled.

"They've got to come out," Fred said. "We're their only way out."

The light passed through the trees again.

"Yeah," Slade finally said. "They're not goin' anywhere. And we've still got some work to do."

The boat motor cranked again.

"We'll be back, Jesse!" Slade yelled. "If you want a ride out of here, you better be waitin' on this creek bank. With the money."

We listened to them motor back up the creek for a moment before Jesse took his hand away from my mouth.

"You took Davey's money?" I said.

"It's not his money. We stole it, and now I'm takin' it for my share. I'll give them theirs later."

"We have to give it back. Davey's gonna be in trouble."

"Davey's already in trouble. And there's nothin' we can do about it. Come on, let's get that motor fixed and haul ass."

Jesse stood, shouldered the backpack, and lifted me by my shirt collar.

"God, that thing stinks," he said. "I think I've got the smell on my pants."

I didn't say anything. I couldn't stop thinking about what Slade was going to do, or had done, to Davey for losing the money.

Jesse let go of me and stepped onto the trail again. I stood there, not sure about anything. Then I saw a cigarette lighter flick a few times until it finally glowed. I watched Jesse lower it to the ground. And in the light I made out the ruined face of a man, his mouth open in death, a dried bloody gash on the side of his face, and a jagged scar across his forehead.

34

JESSE LEAPED BACKWARD, CRASHING INTO THE palmettos as he fled from the body.

I stood there, frozen with fear.

"It's a dead guy!" he said. "Holy crap, it's a dead guy!"

"He has a scar," I said.

"I rolled across that thing! I've got it all over me!"

"On his forehead," I said. "He has a scar."

Jesse turned to me. "We never saw this, understand?"

"But—"

"We don't need this. We don't have time for this."

Jesse veered off the trail and went around the dead man.

"It's Davey's dad," I said.

He turned back to me. "Listen, kid. I don't have time for any more of this. It might not be their dad, and even if it was, I don't care. The guy's food for the swamp animals now, and there's nothin' we can do about it."

"Davey told me he had a scar on his forehead."

Jesse stomped back to me and grabbed me by the arm and pulled me forward. "I don't care, you hear me? If we don't leave this place, we're gonna end up just like him. Slade's gonna kill us. So go fix the motor!"

I let him pull me around the dead body.

"He came looking for Davey," I said.

Jesse grabbed me by the shirt and shoved me ahead of him. "Hell with all of them," he said. "I'm goin' home."

I stopped, and he came against me and shoved me forward again. "Go, kid. I'm not gonna tell you again. It's for your own good."

"Drop the money," I said. I didn't plan to say it; the words just came out.

Jesse stopped. "What?"

"Drop the backpack on the trail," I said. "Right here."

He took a step toward me. "If I have to pick you up and carry you to that boat, I will."

"But you won't get me to fix it," I said. I knew that everything I'd done to that point had been nothing. Now it was going to get hard. Now was when I was actually going to do the right thing.

Jesse hesitated. "What in hell is your problem? You realize what Slade's gonna do to both of us?"

I didn't answer.

"I've seen him beat a guy senseless with a tire iron," he said.

"Leave the money here and I'll fix the boat. And you can go."

Jesse studied me for a second.

"Why?" he said. "Why leave the money?"

"Because taking it just makes things worse."

I felt him staring at me in the darkness.

"We're running out of time," I said.

Jesse threw the backpack to the ground and stomped past me. "Stupid kid," he said. "Dumbass kid."

"I'll be there in a second," I said.

I grabbed the backpack and tossed it toward the outline of a tree that I hoped I would recognize later.

I met Jesse back at the boat and waded around to the motor. He came up close behind me and stood watching over my shoulder. I got the shear pin out of my pocket and slid it into its hole drilled through the prop shaft. Then I got the prop off the deck and stuck it on the shaft, seating the pin into the slot on the back of the prop.

"How long's this gonna take?" Jesse said.

"Just give me the nut," I said.

When he handed it over I began screwing it on.

"Now I need the cotter pin," I said, after tightening the nut as hard as I could with the pliers.

Jesse reached in his pocket and got the pin and gave it to me.

"I hid the money," I said. "So don't think about going back for it."

"Slade knows where both of us live. You thought about that? He won't just let us get away with this."

I didn't answer him. I inserted the cotter pin and bent the ends of it so that it wouldn't come loose. Then I backed away.

"We know too much," Jesse said.

"Go ahead," I said.

Jesse chuckled in disbelief. "You're not comin'?"

"No," I said.

"So now you want the money?"

"I don't want the money. I'm going to leave it where Slade can find it. And I'm going to tell Davey that his dad's here."

"Are you a complete idiot? Then what happens?"

"I don't know. I haven't thought that far ahead. But I need to do it for Davey."

"So what about your boat?"

"It's not important."

"I can't just leave you."

"You can't make me go either."

Jesse stared at me for a moment.

"Fine," he said. "We'll leave the money on the creek bank here, and Slade'll find it. You can come with me."

I shook my head. "I have to see Davey."

Jesse took a deep breath and stared up the creek.

"You better get going," I said.

He turned back to me. "Maybe it's best that I don't have the money," he said. "Now Slade won't have any reason to come after me. I'm out of all this before it gets too bad. Before the cops show up. Maybe I can start over."

Suddenly Jesse didn't seem like he was so much older than I was.

"Maybe," I said.

"And you'll tell your dad that I tried to help."

"Yeah," I said. "I'll tell him. I know you didn't want any of this to happen. You were the only one who was nice to Davey."

Jesse glanced at the ground. "I'm really no better than them," he said.

"Well, like you said, maybe you can start over."

He looked at me and hesitated like he was gradually realizing something. "No," he finally said. "Once you start, you can't really stop. It's best to steer clear of people like me. We'll always let you down in the end."

There was nothing left to say.

Jesse pushed the *Bream Chaser* out into the creek and climbed in. "You sure about this?" he asked.

"Yeah," I said. "I'm sure."

"All right," he said.

He started the motor and looked at me once more before he sped out into the river and into the darkness.

35

I STOOD BY MYSELF ON THE CREEK BANK. THE
insects and night animals thought they were alone again, and
their humming and cheeping and chattering closed around
me. After a moment I turned and stepped toward the trees,
and the night creatures ducked away again. I made my way to
where I'd tossed the backpack and felt in the grass until I
touched it. I thought of the dead body not far from me and
quickly shut the thought away. I got the pack and took it out to
the creek bank and hung it on a limb where it could be easily
seen. Then I turned and stepped into the trees once more.

My biggest concern was getting to the camp through the
swamp in the darkness. I gambled on the animal trail taking
me there, figuring that Davey's dad had known where he was
headed. The trail seemed to run parallel to the creek, just
inside the wall of underbrush. Like a secret, hidden path pigs
and deer had used since the beginning of time. If all else
failed, I could wade along the outside edges of the creek, but
I knew I needed to stay back from the water if I was to avoid
moccasins and alligators.

I thought about Jesse's words: *Then what?*

Then I'd tell Davey about his father. So he wouldn't think his dad never cared. So he'd know his dad came looking for him. He couldn't live without knowing that. I didn't think I could live without telling him.

Then what?

Then I just didn't know. And I didn't want to think about it so much that I'd change my mind. The only thing I was sure of was that Davey had to know about his dad.

I found the trail again and this time turned to my right, back toward the camp. The dead body was somewhere behind me, and I was glad I didn't have to pass it again. But as I got farther away I allowed thoughts of the dead man to creep back into my head. And I wondered how he'd died. I remembered that Officer Stockton had found the boat floating in the river and I thought about the deadhead, and then it all made sense.

Davey's dad had hit the deadhead just like me. And it threw him out of the boat. Just like Jesse.

But how did he die?

I thought for a second he might have drowned, but that didn't make sense since he'd somehow made it into the woods.

Maybe he'd been snakebit. Maybe he'd died of thirst or starvation. There was the blood. Maybe he'd hit his head.

Then I realized it didn't matter. I'd find out eventually. The important thing was that he'd come. He'd tried to find Davey.

I stopped and listened. I couldn't see the creek, but I heard the steady cheeping of frogs, which told me I was still close to the water. And I was surprised that I knew these things, that I had some natural sense of how to go about things out here. I started ahead again, moving slowly, keeping my hands out before me, feeling my way through the darkness. I wasn't scared of spiders or snakes or alligators. I wasn't scared of Slade. I wasn't scared of anything, because I knew I was doing the right thing.

Then what?

Then it didn't matter.

It was impossible to tell how much farther I had to go. I kept on, hearing the frogs to my right, and I was confident that I'd get there eventually. The trail remained underfoot like it had been put there just for me. Like the deadhead. The swamp guiding me to an inevitable end.

Then I heard them. Distant conversation and the dull thud of things being thrown into their boat. I quickened my pace, suddenly worried that they'd leave before I got there. I knew that if I didn't see Davey now, I'd never see him again. It was like he came from nowhere and would go straight back to nowhere.

"Put it up front," I heard Slade say.

Something else thudded into the boat, and I reasoned Slade and Fred were loading their gear.

"Where we gonna sit?" Fred said.

"Sit on top of it," Slade said. "Who cares?"

I came to a dip in the path and stopped. I stepped to my left and felt the trail continuing deeper into the swamp. Then I stepped to my right and it continued toward the creek. I'd intersected their trail to the marijuana field.

I turned and faced the faint opening in the underbrush. I saw the shimmering surface of the creek beyond. I started to think over what I was doing one last time, then decided it was better not to waste time thinking.

They were so busy loading the boat that they didn't hear me approach. I stood in the grass at the edge of the camp, watching them. I didn't see Davey, but I saw Slade and Fred tossing what must have been plastic garbage sacks of marijuana plants into the boat where there was already a big pile of them. Then I saw Davey step out of the camp with a flashlight and a sleeping bag under his arm.

"Davey," I called out.

They all stopped what they were doing and turned to me. Davey didn't act surprised at all. He just looked tired.

Slade threw the bag he was holding onto the pile and came

up onto the deck and stared down at me. "I guess you need a ride?"

"Davey," I said again.

But Davey didn't move or change his expression.

"Where's the money?" Slade said.

"Jesse's gone," I said.

"Gone where?"

"He took my boat. He left the money where you could find it."

Slade turned and looked at Davey. "Lucky you," he said. Then he turned back to me. "I guess he left you, too."

"No, I told him I was staying. I came back to talk to Davey."

Slade turned and looked at his stepbrother. Then he laughed. "Fred," he said, "I really don't know who gets the dumbass award this week."

"Seriously," Fred said.

"I-I found the dead body, Davey," I said.

"Dead body?" Fred said.

"It's the person they've been looking for, Davey," I continued. "You know, they found his boat. And he's been missing since a couple of weeks ago."

Davey nodded slowly like he thought it was something I was happy about and he couldn't help being happy for me.

"Your pal's lost his mind," Slade said.

I kept watching Davey's face. "He's got a scar on his fore-head," I said.

Davey dropped the sleeping bag he was holding.

"It's your dad, Davey. He's the guy they've been looking for . . . But he was looking for you. He came out here looking for you."

"I think he's serious, Slade," Fred said.

"Kid, if you don't stop makin' this stuff up, I'm gonna come down there and knock your head off."

Davey studied me. "Sam wouldn't lie to me," he said quietly.

"Shut up, Davey!" Slade snapped.

Davey looked at his stepbrother. "Why did you do this to me?"

"I don't have time for this. Put what's left in there and get into the boat."

"You told me he didn't love me."

"Get in the boat, Davey," Slade demanded.

"Why did you tell me that?"

"Hey, he said he was comin' out here to get you. That's all I know."

"You don't even care," Davey said.

"He wasn't *my* dad, remember? He was just some man Mom married and they never got along from day one. So you're right. I don't care what happened to him. You satisfied now?"

Davey stared at his stepbrother like he couldn't believe

what he was hearing. "He wouldn't have died if you hadn't made me come out here."

"Get in the boat, Davey."

Davey didn't move.

Slade stepped over to him and grabbed him by the arm. "Get in the boat!"

Davey jerked away from him and backed toward the edge of the deck, just over me.

"I'll leave you out here," Slade warned. "You got five seconds."

Davey's expression suddenly changed, like he could finally see something that had been hazy and blurry. "You're going to leave me anyway," he said.

Slade studied him and didn't say anything. But the silence was just as good as a spoken answer. Davey turned and leaped past me into the marsh. He scrambled to his feet and fled into the swamp. It surprised all of us, and no one made a move to go after him.

"What now?" Fred said.

Slade stared over my head where the trail disappeared into the trees. Then he bent down and picked up the sleeping bag and started toward the boat with it.

"He's not even my brother anyway."

"We can't just leave him."

"I'm not his guardian," Slade mumbled. Then he tossed the sleeping bag into the boat. "Get in, Fred."

Fred pointed to me. "What about him?"

"You want to go to jail, Fred?" Slade shouted.

Fred shook his head.

"Then get in the boat!"

Fred sighed reluctantly before stepping onto the gunnels and climbing on top of the marijuana sacks. He sank down into the heap and stared at me helplessly. Slade started the engine and backed away from the dock. Then he gunned the engine, and the boat roared away down the creek.

36

I TURNED TO THE DARK WALL OF TREES AS THE
night sounds gathered around me once again.

"Davey?" I said softly.

The cicadas and frogs and crickets went silent. I waited
for his reply—nothing.

I had no idea how far he had gone back there. All I knew
was that it had to be after midnight and there was no one else
for miles and nobody coming. I looked down at my watch
and saw that the face of it was shattered. I reasoned I'd hit it
against the boat when we'd slammed into the deadhead.

I climbed onto the deck and went inside the camp, searching for a flashlight. It was too dark to see anything, but it
already sounded hollow. I crossed the room, kicking a few
beer cans and some other trash left on the floor. I felt about
the kitchen counter, touching Baldy's pot and the old coffee-
maker. Then I felt the box of matches I'd brought for Davey.
I opened it and struck one and was amazed at how much just
that little flame burned through the inky darkness. Davey's
jugs lay neatly stored against the wall like he expected to come

back. The bunk beds were bare. The camp looked as empty and lifeless as it had the first day I met Davey.

I shoved the matches into my pocket and went outside again. I thought about the flare and reasoned that I was too far away from help to use it. Even if someone saw it, they wouldn't know where to come.

"Davey," I said again.

But I knew he wouldn't answer, and the fearlessness I'd carried not thirty minutes before was gone. Now the sound of my own voice against the night frightened me. But what scared me even more was the thought of what I had to do. I had to go find Davey. Somewhere out there.

An owl hooted from the inky depths of the swamp, emphasizing the enormity of it all. I dropped into the marsh and started up the trail. When I entered the trees I stopped and struck a match. The giant cavern of darkness sucked the light away like it was an insult. I waved out the flame and found I could see better without it.

I'd been on the trail before, so I wasn't worried about where it went and I knew it was clear of obstructions at least as far as the marijuana field. I followed the path, feeling the gap in palmettos and listening to them rasp against my shorts. For the first time I noticed that my legs were stinging and I reached down and felt them slippery with blood. The palm fronds were slicing into my skin and reopening wounds I must have gotten earlier in the night. My muscles were growing weary. My body was working against me, trying to make me stop. And I began to get confused.

What if he isn't back here?

What if he's just hiding behind the camp?

But deep down I knew better, and I blanked my thoughts and kept on.

I knew I'd reached the field when the palmettos were no longer slicing across me and I looked up and saw the opening in the canopy. With the little light that was falling from the sky, I saw the ground torn and bits of Slade's plants strewn about.

"Davey?" I said.

The owl called again, the only answer I was going to get. And I knew Davey had gone farther. He was going until he couldn't go any more. I didn't want to think about what that meant.

I passed the marijuana field and slowed when the woods got dark again. Now I didn't know the trail or what lay beyond. It made me feel better to think of deer and pigs traveling it in the daytime, like it was their private road. To think of some kind of life in this place, even if it was hidden and unfriendly. Dad had once tried to comfort me about being scared of the dark.

"It's the same thing as daytime," he'd said, "except you can't see."

And it helped to think of it that way. To imagine there was nothing around you except the same things you would see if it were daytime.

The trail began to grow soggy underfoot, and I heard my tennis shoes slurping in a thin coating of mud. I had an idea and stopped and got out the matches. I knelt and struck one and held it close to the ground. There before me were the imprints of Davey's bare feet. I suddenly felt better that I was on the right path and was no longer alone in this place. With new energy I stood again and kept on.

A sharp crack echoed against the stillness. It sounded like a stick breaking. Then I heard splashing

"Davey!" I yelled, my voice booming across the swamp like it was an abandoned church.

Whatever it was began running through the water like it was shallow. The swamp canopy was thinner and it was easier to see. I thought I saw a frothy white disturbance far out in front of me. Then I heard a splash and then running again. It crossed my mind that maybe I was hearing a startled deer or pig. But I knew it wasn't either of those. I knew it was Davey out there.

"Stop, Davey!"

But he kept on, cracking through more tree limbs. Then the splashing stopped and I heard the distant swirl of the water.

I began walking swiftly toward the sound, eventually feeling my tennis shoes slap into the shallows. I realized I was at the edge of a cypress pond, the black shimmering water stretching on both sides of me as far as I could see. I kept on, splashing across it, weaving through the cypress knees, trying to keep my eyes on the last place I'd seen him.

"They're gone!" I called out. "Everybody's gone!"

I didn't hear the splashing anymore, but the sound of my own feet hitting the water was so loud that I thought maybe I just couldn't hear over it.

"It's just me left!" I shouted.

The water was soon up to my knees, and the mud sucked at my shoes. Then it was too hard to lift my feet above the surface, so I began wading, pushing limbs out of my way, searching for any sign of him.

"Davey!" I shouted again.

37

I STOPPED TO LISTEN AND LOOK. THE OWL CALLED again from farther away. The pond before me faded away into darkness and shadow. Shimmering ripples moved out from me in concentric rings, colliding with other ripples coming from beyond me.

"I'm scared, Davey," I said softly.

"Why'd you come after me?" he said.

I trained my eyes on a tree twenty feet in front of me and saw the outline of him standing next to it.

"Because I was worried about you," I said. "Because I didn't know what you'd do."

"I told you what I'd do."

"Don't talk like that."

"I got nobody now."

"You can come home with me," I said. "There's lots of good people you can live with. Your dad was a good person. You know that now."

Davey didn't answer me.

"Let's get out of the water," I said. "There's probably snakes everywhere."

After a moment he began wading toward me and stopped.

"Where are your glasses?" I said.

"They fell off somewhere. I don't care."

"How can you see anything?"

Davey didn't respond.

"All right," I said. "Just follow me."

I turned and started back the way we'd come, but Davey didn't follow.

"Come on, Davey!"

The owl hooted again in the distance.

"I didn't think you'd come," he said.

"Well, I did."

"I wanted you to," he said, "but I didn't think you would."

"Fine. Will you just come with me now?"

Davey nodded and approached me. I turned away from him and started wading again.

"I don't want to stay in the camp tonight," he said.

"We're not," I said.

"Is Slade gone?"

"Yeah," I said. "He's gone. But he might come back. We'll stay hidden in the woods until we hear search and rescue."

"What makes you think they're comin'?"

"My parents will figure out I'm gone."

"How long?"

I didn't know all the answers, and I didn't have a plan. I wished Davey would stop asking me questions.

"I don't know when they'll come," I said. "It could be to-morrow sometime . . . But they'll come. And I have a flare I can shoot."

I kept wading through the water, waiting for it to get shallow again.

"You'll get in trouble," he said.

"I don't care."

"I hope Jesse doesn't go to jail," he said.

I was glad Davey was starting to think about other things besides whatever he'd had in his head earlier. But I was also getting a sinking feeling that the water should have already been shallower. I stopped and looked up at the trees, trying to find some pattern that I recognized. But it all looked the same.

"He was always nice to me," Davey said.

I didn't want Davey to know I was growing concerned about finding our way out of the water, so I started forward again, slightly changing course to my right.

"This way," I said.

"I'm sorry about the *Bream Chaser*."

"It's okay," I said. "It's just a boat."

The water was getting deeper, and it was all I could do to keep myself calm. I didn't want Davey to talk anymore. I needed to concentrate. I stopped and turned back to him.

"We have to get close to a river or a creek bank. There's no way the helicopters can see us down here."

"Why don't we just get back on the trail? We don't have to go all the way to the camp."

The owl called again, sounding even farther away. I looked up at the trees again. "I don't think I can find the trail," I said. "And now my matches are wet."

But Davey didn't seem to care. "How long do you think it is until mornin'?"

"I don't know," I said. "My watch is broken."

"My dad told me one time to stay where I was if I got lost."

"We can't stay in the middle of this pond. We have to keep going. If we go straight, we'll have to come out somewhere eventually."

Davey didn't answer me.

"Come on," I said.

I picked an unusual-looking treetop in the distance and started forward. Soon the water was above my thighs and I pulled the flare from my pocket and held it so that it wouldn't get soaked through.

"Is that the flare?" Davey asked.

"Yes," I said.

"We might have to swim soon."

"I hope not."

"Are you scared?" he said.

"Yes."

"I'm not. Not anymore."

"Good," I said, moving a tree branch out of my face and looking up into the trees again. "It just all looks the same."

"Yeah," he said. "It's just all the same."

I didn't like the way he said it. Like he didn't care what happened to us. I wanted to get out of that dark cypress pond more than anything I'd ever wanted in my life. I couldn't help but think about alligators floating quietly around us. Snakes hanging in the trees. And there was no way to know how much more of it lay ahead.

38

WHEN THE WATER WAS UP TO MY CHEST I
stopped, my head racing with panic. Something splashed
and swirled to my right.

"We're in trouble, Davey."

"Let's stay here," he said.

"Nobody'll ever find us! Don't you understand that?"

"We can see better when daylight comes. And we can find
a way out."

"See what?" I said. "You can barely see fifty feet through
this swamp. And there's no telling how far we are from land."

"I'll be here with you."

"I don't want to be here anymore. I just want to go home."

"Let's swim," he said.

"What if we can't find shallow water again? There's alligators everywhere."

"Listen," he said.

I tried to calm myself. I took deep breaths.

"You hear that?" he said.

I hadn't heard anything. "What?"

"The owl."

Then I heard it. An owl called from just ahead and to the left. Then another answered from somewhere beyond it.

"Hear it?"

"Yeah," I said.

"When I was at the camp by myself I watched the animals and the birds a lot. There was an owl that came near the water in the early mornin' or right before dark. I watched him because I was worried he might get Baldy."

"So what?"

"He never hunted near the water at night. He always moved back into the trees."

"So you think he's over the land?"

"Yeah."

"He's a long way away," I said.

"It always sounds farther than it is. We can swim."

Paralyzing visions of alligators and snakes and deep water fell over me again.

"We can make it," Davey said.

And I didn't understand why he was suddenly so optimistic.

"What about the flare?" I said. "We have to have it. Search and rescue won't know where to look."

"We can take turns holdin' it out of the water."

"And swim with one arm?"

"Yeah," he said. "We can do it. You have to take off your shoes."

I sighed. I didn't see that we had a choice if we wanted to find land. And the flare was useless under the thick swamp canopy.

Davey pulled up his feet and did a breaststroke past me. I held the flare overhead and kicked off my tennis shoes. Then I pushed off the soft bottom and sidestroked behind him.

"You know which way?" I gasped.

"Toward the owl," he said.

I wasn't sure anymore where the last owl call had come from. Struggling to swim through the pond and keep the flare out of the water was all I could do without having to worry about the direction we were headed. I was going to have to rely on Davey to lead us and find the clearest channel through the limbs and tree trunks.

We had been swimming for some time when I came to Davey holding on to a limb. I grabbed next to him and began resting and catching my breath.

"I'll carry it for a while," he said. "You take the lead."

I didn't answer right away.

"Do you think we've been going straight?" I finally gasped.

"Yeah," he said.

"Have you heard the owl again?"

"It's not far," he said.

I held the flare out to him and he took it.

"Which way?" I said.

Davey pointed into the darkness. "That way. Pick trees ahead of you and swim toward them."

I rested a moment longer, then found a tree in the direction Davey had pointed.

"Okay," I finally said. "Let's go."

I let go of the limb and kicked out. It was a relief to finally use both arms. I breaststroked through the still water with ease, keeping my ears tuned to the sound of Davey paddling behind me.

"You okay?" I said back to him.

"Yeah," he said. "I'm fine."

At one point we came across a group of wood ducks that flushed and cried away into the trees. The racket was terrifying, but there was nothing I could do except struggle to stay afloat and take deep breaths and fight the screaming fear in my head.

"God, Davey," I stammered.

"It's okay," he replied calmly. "It's just ducks."

"I know," I said. "I know."

"Keep goin'," he said.

I must have been swimming for a half hour before I heard Davey call from behind me. I stopped and looked back and saw him standing waist-deep. I lowered my feet, felt mud and leaves beneath, and stood.

"We made it," he said.

I looked ahead. I saw nothing but shimmering water, but it was a relief to be able to stand again, and I reasoned we were probably close to finding land. Davey came up to me and held out the flare.

"Still dry," he said.

I turned and picked out another tree in the distance and started for it. The water grew shallower, and soon it was no higher than our knees. I jumped when a blue heron startled before us and flew away, screaming its raspy alarm.

"We're close," Davey said.

We finally trudged out of the pond and into a thicket of palmettos. I sat against a cypress tree to rest, and Davey sat beside me. He put the flare into my lap.

"I told you we could do it," he said like he was proud of himself.

"That's the scariest thing I've ever done in my life," I said.

"You were always brave," he said. "You just never had to prove it."

I looked up at the sky. It didn't seem like there was any trace of daylight yet.

"We've got to be close to a river," I said. "I don't know which one, but we have to be close to something."

"No way Slade can find us now," Davey said.

"No way anybody can find us," I replied. "We have to keep going."

"I'm ready to go again when you're rested."

"I never heard the owl again," I said. "Not once. I just kept trying to swim straight."

"I made that up."

"Made what up?"

"About the owl bein' over land."

"Seriously?"

"Yeah." Davey laughed. "But it sounded like it would work."

"Geez," I said.

"We had to pick a direction," he said.

I smiled and would have laughed with him if I hadn't been so concerned that we still didn't have any idea where we were.

"Sometimes you can lie if it helps people," he said.

I grabbed the flare and stood. "Come on."

39

I PICKED ANOTHER TREE AND STARTED THROUGH the palmettos toward it with Davey following.

"Stupid owls," I said. "I can't believe you thought of that."

Davey laughed to himself quietly.

We pushed through the underbrush for a couple of hours before dawn seeped through the canopy and the swamp revealed itself in shades of gray. I stopped and looked over my shoulder and saw the sky lighter behind us.

"We're headed west," I said. "The Pascagoula River should be somewhere in front of us. But I thought we'd have gotten to it by now."

"We'll make it," Davey said.

I looked at him. His hair was littered with sticks and leaves. His arms and legs were covered in palmetto cuts. But he smiled at me like he didn't know about or feel any of it.

"At least it's getting daylight," I said.

"I've never stayed up all night before."

"Me neither," I said. "Are you tired?"

He shook his head. "No. Let's keep walkin'. I'll bet we're close."

I was tired. My legs ached and my face and arms burned from the palmetto cuts. I wanted to lie down and sleep. Then I reminded myself that we had to get somewhere we could be found. Somewhere a boat might pass.

As the swamp grew lighter squirrels began to chatter and leap through the treetops. Birds called and flitted about the underbrush. The swamp gradually filled with the comforting sounds of life, even if it was just animal life.

I heard an osprey cheeping from far overhead and I knew the river was ahead of us before I saw it. When I finally stared through the trees at the black water, I felt relief wash over me. I didn't know what part of the river it was, but at least we'd come to the end of that terrible place behind us. I sat on a log and watched Davey approach.

"I told you," he said.

He sat down beside me while I pulled out the flare and studied it.

"Think it'll work?" he asked.

"I don't know. We kept it as dry as we could."

"How do you use it?"

"I'm reading the directions."

"Maybe we should wait until we see somebody," he said. "A boat will probably come along soon."

He was right. We should wait. I looked up again and studied the empty river.

"How come you're not worried about anything anymore?" I said.

"I don't know," he said.

"Are you thinking about your dad?"

"For a while I was tryin' to remember his face. What he looked like."

"I guess it's been a long time since you saw him."

Davey nodded. "Since I was a little kid."

The osprey cheeped again and I looked up and saw it pass over the middle of the river.

"I thought I would be sadder," Davey said.

"You acted pretty upset when you ran off from Slade. I thought you were gonna drown yourself."

"But I don't think I was sad," he said. "I just didn't know what to do anymore. It didn't seem like there was anyplace else to go."

I studied the flare again, not knowing what to say.

"It feels good to finally know."

"Know what?"

"That I won't ever have a dad. That Slade doesn't care about me. That I don't have to think about anybody comin' for me . . . At least now I know."

I started to reply, but then I heard something. A faint buzzing in the distance.

Suddenly Davey leaped up. "I hear a boat!" he said.

I stood. "Yeah," I said.

"Get the flare ready!" he said.

I hurried to the riverbank and looked downriver, where the engine sound was coming from. The boat was still out of sight. Davey came up behind me and peered over my shoulder.

"Hurry!" he said.

But for some reason I hesitated.

"Let's wait until we see it," I said. "Back up."

I heard leaves crunch as Davey took a step back. I kept my eyes trained on the river bend. Then I watched the boat race around the point. To my horror, I saw that it was Slade.

"Run!" I yelled.

But I knew he saw us. He swung the jon to the right and headed straight for us. I spun and ran into Davey.

"Go!" I yelled. "It's Slade!"

Davey didn't move. I looked at him and his face was colorless like the life had gone out of him. I grabbed his arm and pulled at him desperately, but he wouldn't budge. I shoved him and he fell back into the leaves. Then I rushed to him and grabbed his wrist and tried to pull him up.

"Get up!"

He jerked his hand away.

"I can't," he said. "I can't see."

"You can follow me! Get up!"

He shook his head. "That won't work, Sam. I'll just slow us down. You know that."

The roar of Slade's boat was so close it seemed he was about to run us over.

I bent over and tried to grab him again, but he rolled

away and backed against a tree and locked his arms over his chest.

"Go, Sam," he said calmly. "You can come find me again."

I didn't know what to do. I saw Slade's boat in my periphery, bearing down on us, not fifty yards away now.

"If he gets both of us, we don't have a chance," Davey said.

I took a step back.

"Please come find me," he said again.

I nodded. I heard the tone of the outboard change, and then I heard it crash into the underbrush. I turned and ran. I tripped and fell over a cypress knee and dropped the flare. I scrambled to my feet and left it and kept on. I had a sudden thought that maybe Slade had a gun and he was pointing it at my back and the fear of it went white-hot up my spine. I fell again and this time crawled behind a tree and stood and peered around it.

Slade was standing over Davey, not a hundred feet away, watching me. He didn't appear to have a gun. He studied me for a few seconds more, then looked down at Davey.

"Get up!" he commanded.

Davey looked at his knees and shook his head.

Slade kicked him in the shoulder and knocked him over into the leaves.

"Leave him alone!" I yelled.

Slade looked at me. "Why don't you come over here and save him, kid?"

I stepped from behind the tree and faced him.

Slade kept his eyes on me, the creepy doll face boring into me. After a moment he smiled and looked back down at Davey.

"You see," he said. "I'm the only person who cares about you."

Davey said something I couldn't make out.

Slade bent over and grabbed him and pulled him up and shoved him back against the tree. "Look at me!"

But Davey wouldn't look up. He began to tremble. Then he started to lift his hands to his face and Slade slapped them away. Davey sniffled and rubbed his eyes.

"I thought we were family," Slade said. "But I guess you're no better than the rest."

"He doesn't want to go with you!" I shouted. "Just leave him alone!"

Slade looked at me. "Where's the money?"

"I told you. I left it on the creek bank. Hanging on a tree."

He continued to study me.

"We don't have it," I said. "How could we have it?"

Then I knew. Jesse had come back and found the money. He couldn't help himself.

Slade turned to Davey again. "Get in the boat," he said.

"Jesse's got the money!" I said.

Slade pulled Davey from the tree and shoved him toward the boat. Then he turned back to me. "And now I've got insurance that you'll keep your mouth shut. You say a word about anything you've seen or heard out here, and I'll kill him and dump him with his dad."

I froze. I couldn't make words in my mouth. I realized that I was face-to-face with true evil, and I was nothing up against it.

Slade looked at the ground and saw the flare. He stepped over to it and picked it up. Then he tossed it into the river as he started for the boat. I saw that Davey was already sitting on the front seat. I stood there helplessly as Slade climbed past him, started the engine, and backed away. When I heard the motor shift into forward gear it somehow snapped me out of my state and I began running toward them.

"I'll get you more money!" I yelled. I didn't know where the idea had come from, but it was all I could think of.

I broke from the trees and splashed into the river until the water was up to my chest. The boat was already racing away. I saw Davey in the front seat with his back to me.

"Davey!" I yelled.

He didn't turn around.

40

I WATCHED AS SLADE'S BOAT RACED AWAY toward the first bend in the river, and I was certain that I wouldn't see Davey again. I'd never felt such a sense of helplessness, and I began coughing like I wanted to cry but there were no tears. I tried to yell again, even though I knew it was useless. I bent over and rested my hands on my knees and coughed at the water, then looked up again and stared after them.

Just as Slade was about to turn out of sight I saw another boat roar around the bend and pass him. I stopped coughing and stared at it like it was only something in my imagination. Officer Stockton's patrol boat slowed while Slade's jon slammed into his wake and clattered over it.

I stood up and raised my arms slowly. Then I began to believe what I was seeing, and I started waving my hands in the air.

"Over here!" I shouted. "Hey!"

The patrol started to make a slow turn in the middle of the river.

"Help!" I shouted.

The boat slowed and drifted for a moment like the driver was considering going after Slade.

"Help!" I shouted again.

Then it began turning back. Its engine groaned as the vessel dug into the water and lifted and came for me. I watched my father hurry out of the wheelhouse and scramble to the bow.

Dad leaped into the shallows of the river, still wearing his uniform from work. He waded to me and hugged me to his chest.

"Thank God," he said.

The patrol boat backed up beside us and stopped. Officer Stockton came onto the deck and looked down at us.

"You okay, son?" Dad asked.

I nodded against him. "He took him, Dad," I said.

"Let's get him in the boat, Roger," Officer Stockton said with urgency.

Dad let go of me as Officer Stockton reached his hand out and I grabbed it.

"Dad," I said, "my friend's in that other boat. We have to get him."

Officer Stockton lifted me over the gunnels and led me around to the wheelhouse. We went inside, and he pointed to a jump seat against the wall, but I didn't want to sit.

"We have to hurry," I said.

"You know those people?"

"Yes," I said desperately. "It's my friend and his step-brother."

Dad was coming up a ladder at the stern of the boat, dripping wet in his clothes.

"I think that's the boat I've been looking for," Officer Stockton continued.

"It is," I said. "But my friend didn't have anything to do with it. And I think his stepbrother's going to hurt him."

I watched Officer Stockton's face grow tight and stern. "Get in here, Roger," he said.

Dad walked through the wheelhouse door and pulled me to him again. "Just glad you're safe," he said. "I don't even care—"

"Hold on," Officer Stockton interrupted.

The engines roared beneath our feet, and the boat tilted as the stern dug into the water. Dad and I were pressed against the back wall of the wheelhouse.

"We've got to catch them, Dad."

"We'll catch them," Officer Stockton said with confidence.

And once we were racing down the river I had no doubt that we would. I'd never been in a boat so powerful and fast. The riverbank raced by like we were on a highway and I was watching trees out the car window. As we carved the bends in the river, Officer Stockton gently and precisely turned the steering wheel with the palm of his hand and kept his eyes trained on the water ahead. It seemed like only moments later we were running over the frothy white trail of Slade's boat. Then around the next bend was a straight part of the river, and I saw the boat itself.

Dad let go of me and stepped out from against the wall and got next to the wheel. Officer Stockton grabbed his radio handset and keyed the mic.

"Dispatch, this is Unit Two. I'm on the West Pascagoula just south of Crane Lakes. I'm ten-forty-three, in pursuit of a robbery suspect."

"Ten-four, Unit Two. Are you requesting backup?"

"Negative. No backup at this time."

"Ten-four, Unit Two. No backup at this time. We've got your coordinates and will be on standby for further instructions."

Officer Stockton replaced the handset, keeping his eyes on Slade's boat.

"How you wanna do this, Jim?" Dad asked.

Officer Stockton reached overhead and flipped a switch on the ceiling. I heard a siren wail from the roof, and the insides of the gunnels strobed with blue and white light.

"We'll let *him* decide," Officer Stockton said.

Dad glanced at him and nodded.

A moment later Officer Stockton cut the wheel and roared between Slade and the riverbank. Then he slowed the boat until we were running alongside and towering over them. I saw Davey watching us, his eyes wide with fear. Slade looked at us once, his doll face emotionless and evil-looking, then he set his sights on the river again, as much as saying there was no way he was going to surrender.

Officer Stockton grabbed another mic from the ceiling and spoke into it. I heard his voice boom from a loudspeaker on the roof.

"Pull your vessel over and shut off your engine!"

Slade ignored him.

"Sam?" Officer Stockton said over his shoulder.

"Sir?" I said.

"Do you know if he has a gun?"

"I haven't seen him with one, but I don't know."

Officer Stockton nodded. "Roger," he said, "take that AR-15 off the wall, unload it, and get on the deck with it."

Dad turned and removed the assault rifle from its rack. He pulled the clip, dropped it in his pocket, and worked the action, making sure there wasn't a shell in the chamber. Then he turned to me and said, "Stay inside."

I nodded.

Officer Stockton shoved down on the throttle, and we raced ahead of Slade's boat. Dad left the wheelhouse and walked up to the bow, holding a handrail with one hand and the assault rifle with the other. After a moment he steadied himself at the front window and turned back to look at us. He gave

Officer Stockton a nod. I felt the boat lean into a turn, and I grabbed hold of a strap on the ceiling and hung there. Then the patrol boat slowed and sat down in the water. We were sideways in the channel, with Slade's boat bearing down like it would ramp over us. Dad stepped to the center of the bow, brought the assault rifle to his shoulder, and leveled it right at them.

It's not loaded, Davey, I thought to myself, like maybe he could hear me.

Even with an AR-15 pointed at his head, it didn't appear Slade was going to slow. I watched Davey grab one side of the boat and scoot over to it like he was thinking of jumping out. It suddenly crossed my mind that Slade was going to kill both of them.

"Come on," Officer Stockton mumbled. "Think about it."

I saw his hand pressed against the throttle, ready to shove it forward in an instant. Dad stepped closer to the railing and re-shouldered the rifle with emphasis. Slade's boat was going to hit us dead-on in seconds.

"Come on," Officer Stockton said again, with more urgency in his voice.

At the last instant it must have crossed Slade's mind that he didn't want to kill himself. He slowed and shoved the tiller hard to his left. But it was too late. They were too close and going too fast.

Officer Stockton turned and yanked me to him and

squeezed me tight against his hip. His free hand darted up and grabbed another overhead strap.

"Hold on!" he yelled.

I saw Dad drop to the deck and disappear from my sight. Then there was a loud, hollow, metallic bang that rocked the patrol boat.

41

OFFICER STOCKTON SHOVED ME ASIDE AND dashed out of the wheelhouse. I saw Dad on his feet again, and then both of them were leaning over the side of the patrol boat. I rushed to the window and watched as they pulled Slade from below and rolled him over the gunnels. They flopped him onto the deck, and Officer Stockton pinned him with one knee on his back, already reaching for his handcuffs. Dad straightened and searched the river as he kicked off his shoes. The wrecked jon boat appeared, drifting away from us. Davey wasn't in it.

"You see him, Roger?"

"No!"

"He ejected! I saw him eject!" Officer Stockton yelled.

Dad turned in a circle, inspecting the water all around us.

"I don't see him, Jim!"

Officer Stockton left Slade facedown on the deck, cuffed and moaning. He hurried to the stern and searched the water.

"Got him!" Dad shouted.

Dad vaulted the railing and I saw water splash above the

gunnels. Officer Stockton spun and grabbed a throw ring hanging outside the wheelhouse. He rushed to the bow, hesitated, then hurled it in Dad's direction. It was attached to a rope, and he held on to the end as the rest uncoiled. Then I saw Davey floating facedown in the river and Dad swimming for him. Dad turned him over and got behind him and put his arm around his chest. Then he sidestroked the limp body to the throw ring and grabbed hold. Officer Stockton began pulling them to us.

I came out of the wheelhouse, wanting to help. I stood behind Officer Stockton as he dragged Davey over the stern and laid him on the deck. Davey's eyes were closed and his face was pale. Officer Stockton knelt over him, tilted his head back, and began performing mouth-to-mouth resuscitation. He blew into him twice, then straightened and used the palms of his hands to pump Davey's chest.

Dad came up the ladder and stood over us. I felt a hand on my shoulder.

"Don't let him die," I said.

Officer Stockton continued to pump Davey's chest and study his face. "Breathe, kid," he said.

I remembered what Davey had told me about seeing his dead mother. That you could tell nobody was in there. That she was gone. And that's what I thought, looking at him. That Davey wasn't in there.

Officer Stockton pumped at Davey's chest again, more

forcefully this time and with a growing sense of urgency. "Breathe, dammit!" he said.

"Dad?" I said quietly.

He didn't answer me.

"Dad, is he—"

Davey's body suddenly convulsed as the boy coughed and spit up water. Officer Stockton grabbed his head and turned it sideways and stuck his finger into Davey's mouth. Then Davey was coughing up more water and color flooded his face. Dad squeezed my shoulder and I felt relief wash over me.

"There you go," Officer Stockton said. "Cough it up, kid."

Davey's eyes opened and he wheezed and drew his knees up.

"Just take it easy," Officer Stockton said.

Davey looked about, his eyes foggy and glazed over. He was taking deep breaths and his chest was rising and falling rapidly. Then he saw me and coughed again and smiled.

"Sam," he said.

I laughed nervously. "Hey, Davey."

Officer Stockton rocked back on his heels and rubbed his face with his hand. Davey coughed again, keeping his eyes on me.

"Did I almost die?" he said.

"Yeah," I said.

"Did you get in trouble?"

I laughed again. "Not yet," I said.

Officer Stockton put his hand behind Davey's shoulder

and helped him sit up. "Just rest here for a few minutes, Davey. Does your chest hurt?"

"A little," he said.

"Okay. I don't think I broke a rib, but you're going to be sore. Sam, why don't you stay back here with him while I get us to the dock."

"Sure," I said.

"Keep your mouth shut, Davey!" Slade shouted. I was surprised to hear him speak. Davey looked to his right and seemed to notice him for the first time.

"Roger, you wanna keep an eye on that other fellow?" Officer Stockton said.

"No problem," Dad said. "Is that your brother, Davey?"

Davey studied Slade for a moment. "He's not my real brother," he said. "I barely know him."

42

IN ALL OF THE CONFUSION THERE HADN'T BEEN
time to tell Dad anything about what had happened. Then
Officer Stockton was driving us back to the marine police dock
and the engines were too loud to talk over. Dad stood guard
over Slade, glancing back at me and Davey occasionally.

When we got to the dock some of Dad's police officers were
there to take Slade. There were also two S&R boats tying up
like they had just come in from the south. Slade looked back at
Davey once before the officers dragged him off, but it was
more of a warning than anything else. Davey glanced at him,
then turned away.

"You want to tell my dad about the rest?" I asked him.

Davey looked at me. "You can tell him," he said. "It's okay."

Dad was helping Officer Stockton tie the mooring lines
when I approached him. "There's a dead body out there," I
said.

Davey remained at his spot in the stern while I sat inside
the wheelhouse with Dad and Officer Stockton. I told them

everything about the swamp camp and the marijuana, and I told them where Davey's dad was. As my story unfolded, Officer Stockton took notes and Dad watched me with disbelief.

"I just wanted to do something brave," I said.

Dad nodded, still trying to wrap his head around all that had happened.

"And then I didn't know how to tell anybody about it," I said.

"You could have gotten yourself killed, Sam," Dad said. But his words were more him considering it to himself than a lecture.

"I know," I said. "It just got out of control."

"We started looking for you last night. We got it out of Grover that you'd gone out in your boat, but he didn't know where. S&R's been all over south of here. We never imagined you'd be up in the management area."

I looked at the floor. I didn't know what else to say.

"Then early this morning Grover mentioned something about a camp. And that's when I remembered you asking me about that place. So Jim and I decided to run upriver."

I smiled. "Thanks, Grover," I said, only half sarcastically.

Dad hugged me to his shirt and rubbed my back. He didn't mention all the lies or losing my boat. But I believed for the first time in my life that he was proud of me.

"Let's get you and your friend to the house," he said.

• • •

We helped Davey off the patrol boat and up to Dad's Tahoe. Officer Stockton said he'd come by the house and check on us later. The S&R crew was readying their gear again, and he was going to guide them upriver to recover the body and inspect the swamp camp.

"I'm sorry about causing all the trouble," I said.

"Well, I think you've learned more lessons than we've got time to go into right now," Officer Stockton said. "I'm glad you two came out of it okay." He turned to Dad. "Go get them cleaned up, Roger. I guess you'll handle Davey's situation from here?"

"Thanks, Jim. I'll handle it. If he complains about his chest for more than a couple of days, I'll get it checked out."

"Good," Officer Stockton said. "I had to get pretty rough with him."

Dad reached out and they shook hands. "Hey," Dad said, "I couldn't have done better."

Officer Stockton nodded and turned to go. He lifted a finger into the air and waved it over his shoulder.

I opened the back door of Dad's Tahoe and told Davey to climb in. I got in behind him and shut the door again. When I looked over he was sitting up straight and smiling to himself.

"What?" I said.

"Nothing," he said.

I guessed he'd probably never been in a car that nice, much less a police car. "It's faster than the regular ones," I said.

"Cool," Davey said.

Dad got in and pulled his door shut.

"Buckle up, boys," he said.

Davey grabbed his seat belt and jerked it out and snapped it quickly into the buckle. Then he faced forward, grabbed the door handle, and braced himself.

"It's not like that," I said.

He looked at me and laughed. Then I started laughing, too, and neither of us could look at each other without cracking up. Dad cocked his eyes at us in the rearview mirror, grinned, and shook his head.

When we got home Mom was waiting for us in the driveway. She hugged me tightly; it felt good, and I wasn't the least bit embarrassed about it. After a while she let go and I turned back to Davey, who was standing patiently behind me.

"This is Davey," I said. "He's my friend I found in the swamp."

Mom raised her eyebrows and studied him. "Really?" she said.

And I realized Dad hadn't had a chance to call her and explain everything. He walked up to her and said, "It's a long story, sweetheart."

"It sounds like it," she said. "You boys look awful. How did you get so many cuts?"

"I think we'd better get them inside and cleaned up," Dad said. "Then they can tell you all about it over lunch."

We went inside the house, and Dad told me to show Davey

my room and told both of us to take showers while he called to check on things at the office. Davey followed me down the hall and into my room.

"This is nice," Davey said.

"It's all right," I said.

I watched Davey looking around, taking in everything.

"We need to get you some more glasses," I said.

"Yeah," he said. "And maybe some shoes."

"You need, like, everything."

"Wish we had some of that money."

"It was stolen. We couldn't keep it."

"Well, I didn't know it," he said.

"Yes you did. You just didn't want to believe it."

Davey looked at me. "I just didn't want to believe any of it."

"I know. My parents'll buy you what you need. It's no big deal."

I heard the phone ringing, and then Mom called me.

"Grover's on the phone," she said.

"Okay," I said.

"Your friend?" Davey said.

"Yeah," I said. "I'll be right back. You can go ahead and take a shower in my bathroom."

"Okay," he said.

I went into the kitchen, where Mom was fixing lunch. The smell of meatloaf and mashed potatoes was already flowing throughout the house. She studied me and shook her head.

"You and your friend need to swab those cuts with alcohol."

"We will," I said. "I just need to talk to Grover first."

I picked the handset off the counter and walked into the living room with it.

"Hey," I said.

"I thought you'd died."

"I almost did. Glad you finally told them where I was."

"I told them what I *knew*! Which was close to zero!"

"I know, Grover. Geez, I'm just kidding."

"I'd come see you, but it's hard to get up."

"I know."

"So when are you coming over?"

"I just got home, Grover."

"So?"

"So, like, my parents are happy that I'm alive and everything and they probably want me to stick around for lunch at least."

"How long's that going to take?"

"I don't know. And Davey's over here and we're cleaning him up and feeding him."

"That sounds like you found a dog."

"You know what I mean."

"What are you going to do after that?"

"I'll come over as soon as I can."

"I mean, what are you going to do with him?"

"We haven't figured it out yet."

"Are you going to find him a place to live?"

"I guess. But it's not like we can just put an ad in the paper for him."

"Bring him over here when you come so I can meet him."

"Okay," I said. "I'll call you later."

"Okay," he said.

I started to hang up, then stopped myself.

"Grover!" I said.

"What?"

"Thanks for checking on me."

"You're welcome," he said.

43

WHEN I GOT BACK TO MY ROOM DAVEY WAS already finished with his shower and standing in the middle of the floor with a towel around his waist. I set the alcohol and cotton swabs on my dresser.

"That was fast," I said.

"I didn't wanna use all the hot water," he said.

"We've got tons of hot water."

"I didn't know," he said.

I told Davey he could take longer in the shower, but he said he was already clean. Then I told him to disinfect his cuts and get what he wanted to wear out of my dresser drawers.

When I came out he was standing in the same place waiting for me, this time dressed in a pair of my old shorts and a T-shirt.

"This okay?" he said.

"Whatever you want," I said.

"Your mom must be a good cook," he said. "It smells really good."

"She is," I said. "And I'm starving. Let me get dressed and we'll eat."

I started for my dresser to grab some clothes for myself.

"Sam?" he said.

I stopped and faced him again.

"I think I'm about to fall down."

"What?"

"I'm really tired. But your mom fixed lunch and every-thing."

"It's okay," I said. "Get in my bed and sleep. You can eat later."

"I can sleep on the floor," he said.

"No, use my bed."

Davey was too tired to argue. He walked to my bed and lay on top of it. He pulled my pillow under his head and closed his eyes.

I pulled on some shorts and another T-shirt. Just talking about sleep had made me realize I was tired, too. Suddenly there was nothing I wanted more than to lie down and sleep next to him.

As I was hanging my towel in the bathroom I heard Mom knock gently on my door. I walked out and opened it. She looked past me at Davey on the bed.

"He's too tired to eat," I said quietly.

She came in and got a blanket off the end of the bed and put it over him. She watched him for a moment. "It's okay," she said. "Let him sleep."

"I'm pretty tired, too," I said.

She put her hand on my back, guided me out of the room,

and pulled the door behind us. "Go get into our bed," she said. "Lunch can wait."

I woke in Mom and Dad's bed that evening. Daylight was fading outside the window, and I heard birds cheeping and squirrels fussing in the treetops. I didn't remember having ever slept so soundly.

I got up and walked into the sunroom, where Mom was working on a new painting. She set her paintbrush down and wiped her hand on a dishcloth.

"Feeling better?" she said.

I nodded. "A lot. Davey up yet?"

"No. He's still sleeping. I checked on him a few minutes ago. Your father should be home shortly. He went back to the precinct."

I sat on a small sofa beneath the window and rubbed my eyes. I knew the talk was coming.

"Your father told me most of it," she said.

I looked at the floor and nodded.

"Please don't make me worry about you like that again."

"I won't," I said.

Mom let the silence sink into me for a moment.

"Thank you," she finally said. "I don't suppose there's really anything else I can say, Sam. I guess you must have more of your father in you than I thought. You make doing the wrong thing seem right . . . somehow."

I took that as her approval. I smiled and looked at her.

She wasn't smiling. "But don't do it again," she repeated firmly.

I frowned and nodded that I understood. Then I looked out the window and studied the fireflies floating in the gloam.

"Mom, do you think you can help Davey?"

"I've already made some calls. It's going to take time to figure out the best situation for him, but your father and I will do whatever we can."

I heard the front door open.

"There's your dad now," she said, standing.

We met Dad in the kitchen, where he was grabbing a beer out of the refrigerator. He straightened and saw me, and I could tell by the look on his face that he had something good to tell us.

"You're alive again," Dad joked.

"Shhh," Mom said.

Dad glanced in the direction of my room.

"He's still asleep," I said.

Dad widened his eyes and nodded. Mom moved past him and began pulling the meatloaf from the oven, where she'd been keeping it warm.

"Well," Dad said to me quietly, "Jim found your boat. Looks to be in good shape. It was tied up at the launch at the end of Roys Road. We'll go get it in the morning."

I felt another layer of relief settle over me.

"Did they find Jesse and Fred?" I asked.

"Not yet, but my guys say they know where each of them lives. That Slade fellow got to talking once they told him how much trouble he was facing."

"How about Davey's dad?"

"They found him," he said. "Jim thinks maybe it was a heart attack. The coroner's going to let us know."

"Will he have a funeral?"

"Yeah, we'll get all that worked out. Davey holding up okay?"

"He's been sleeping all afternoon." I turned to Mom. "I guess I ought to wake him."

She nodded. "Go ahead," she said. "You boys need to eat."

Davey sat small and unsure of himself at the table. While Dad said the blessing he stared at his plate. Then Davey glanced at me, and he looked so funny that I thought I was going to laugh out loud. He smiled and quickly looked away again.

Dad passed around the meatloaf and mashed potatoes and other sides, and I saw Davey watching to see how we did things, then he did them the same way, taking the same portions. It wasn't until we began eating that both of us lost any self-control. We shoveled our food down like we were in a race.

"Take it easy, boys," Dad said.

But I could tell he wasn't really concerned. He and Mom watched us and smiled at each other.

"It's really good," Davey said, chewing.

"They found the *Bream Chaser*," I mumbled, with my mouth full.

Davey's eyes got wide with excitement and he nodded. He stuffed in another bite. "Good," he said.

We cleaned our plates, and Mom passed everything around to us again.

No one said much of anything else until we were halfway through our second helpings and starting to slow. Mom and Dad had both finished by then, and they were waiting and watching us patiently.

"Davey," Mom said, "I told Sam earlier that I made a few calls for you today. Our church has a social services group that can help locate a family for you."

Davey glanced at me.

"They picked out a bad one for him last time," I said. "I think he's worried about that."

"Well, our group doesn't work that way," Mom said. "You get to interview the family first, and if you don't think you want to live with them, then you don't have to."

Davey looked up at her. "You mean, *I* get to pick?"

"That's right," Mom said. "And I'm going to get involved with the interviews myself to make sure we find a family you're comfortable with."

Davey studied her for a moment. "Where will I stay while I make sure?" he said.

I looked at Mom.

She looked at Dad.

Dad shrugged.

"I don't see why you can't stay here," Mom said. "If that's fine with you, Sam?"

"Awesome!" I said.

Davey smiled, pleased with himself.

"Davey," Dad continued, "they found your father's body. They're going to figure out what happened. Do you know if he had heart issues?"

I watched Davey, wondering how he'd react to thoughts of his dad.

He shook his head like he didn't mind thinking of it. "I don't know," he said. "I don't remember."

Dad nodded considerately. "Well, we'll get some answers. And we'll have a proper funeral."

"Okay," Davey said.

44

AFTER SUPPER DAVEY AND I WENT BACK TO MY
room. I told him to sit on the floor in front of the television.
I flipped on the Xbox and sat beside him with the game controller.

"Video games," he said, like it was something he'd only
seen a few times before.

"Yeah," I said. "We'll see what Grover's up to."

We waited while the game loaded.

"I always wondered what you were doing," Davey said. "I
thought about where you were. I didn't know it would be this
nice."

"We'll go over to Grover's house tomorrow," I said. "Then
you'll really see nice."

"Wonder how long I'll get to live here?" he said.

"I don't know. Mom said sometimes it can take a while to
find a family."

"Maybe nobody will want me," he said.

I looked at him. He was about to laugh, and I knew what
he meant. We both cracked up at his joke.

"Yeah," I said. "That wouldn't be so bad."

He shook his head. "No, it wouldn't."

The game loaded and I typed in my password, *Bream Chaser12*.

"I'll bet Grover's mad at me right now," I said.

"Why?"

"Well, not really. But he doesn't have a lot of patience. Watch."

I submitted the password, and we were suddenly staring at a screen full of messages. Davey squinted his eyes and scooted closer to the television screen.

Hello?

Sam!

I'm calling your house again if you don't answer me in 10 seconds.

10 . . . 9 . . . 8 . . . 7 . . . 6 . . . 5 . . . 4 . . . 3 . . . 2 . . . 1

. . . Sam?

I laughed. "He's getting better," I said. "You want to type something to him?"

Davey looked at me like he wasn't completely sure of the joke. He shook his head. I started typing a reply to Grover. "We'll see how he's doing," I said. "And introduce you. He wants to know all about you."

• • •

We never got to play any video games. We spent nearly an hour messaging back and forth with Grover, giving him details of our adventure. Davey didn't type any of the messages himself, but it didn't take him long to get a sense of Grover's personality through the types of questions he asked and his explosive reaction to our responses. Eventually Davey began suggesting things for me to type.

"Tell him I drink five-year-old Dr Pepper."

I typed it.

Grover responded immediately.

> What? Does he want to die? Where do you even GET five-year-old Dr Pepper?!

Davey and I couldn't stop laughing.

Dad brought one of our camping cots into my room and set it up beside my bed. Then Mom brought an extra pillow and blankets. I offered Davey my bed, but he insisted on taking the cot. Even though we'd slept that afternoon, both of us were getting tired again by ten o'clock. Mom came in once more to make sure we were comfortable in our beds, then she turned off the light and left us alone. We were still giggling from our chat session with Grover.

"It's really hard for him to believe some of this stuff," I said.

"Slade really wouldn't have liked him," Davey said.

I laughed again. "No. Slade would *not* have liked him."

Our thoughts took over until we were quiet once more.

"It's all better now, Davey," I finally said.

"Yeah," he said. "I didn't know it could be this good."

"It seems like it was such a waste of time for me to be so worried about that fight I told you about."

"Sometimes you don't know what you should worry about."

"What Mom told me was right. There's just bad people in the world. Sometimes they do bad things to people like us. But it doesn't mean there's anything wrong with us."

"But it makes you *feel* like something might be wrong with you, doesn't it?"

"And when you try to change, it just makes things worse."

"You just have to find the right people," he said.

"Yeah," I said. "And realize who your real friends are."

Neither of us spoke for a moment.

"Sam?"

"Yeah."

"What are we going to do tomorrow?"

"Go get my boat. Go see Grover."

"Okay."

A few more seconds of silence passed.

"Sam?"

"Yeah."

"I can't wait until tomorrow."

45

THE NEXT MORNING DAD TOOK ME AND DAVEY TO
get my boat.

On the way, he asked us if we'd like to go out fishing with
him on Saturday.

Davey's eyes went wide. "Sure," he said.

It was only a couple of miles to the launch at the end of Roys
Road. It was nothing more than a gravel parking area between
a cutout in the riverbank and an abandoned nightclub. I saw
the *Bream Chaser* tied to what was left of a rickety dock.

I got out of Dad's Tahoe carrying two flotation vests, with
Davey coming after me. For some reason he always slid
across the seat and got out behind me instead of using his
own door. Dad took a jerrican out of the back, and the three
of us went down to the boat.

"Looks to be all right," Dad said.

"Yes, sir," I said, looking it over and stepping down into it.

I put the flotation vests on the seat. Dad passed the jerrican
to me and I stepped to the back, uncapped the tank, and began
fueling it. Davey remained on the dock, squinting his eyes

and moving them across the parking lot and up over the old nightclub.

"I've been here before," he said.

Dad looked down at him.

"This is where Slade dropped me off in the canoe," he said.

"My guys picked up Slade's two friends last night," Dad said. "Fred Kern and Jesse Harbison."

"They get the money?" I asked.

Dad nodded. "Yep. And a bunch of dope."

"How long will they go to jail?" Davey asked.

"It might be a while before they get convicted, but I imagine a long time."

Dad studied what I was doing again, watching the jerrican emptying into the tank. It used to make me nervous, him watching me like that, but I didn't mind now.

"Going to pay your old foster parent a visit today, Davey," Dad said.

Davey looked at him.

"Put him in jail, too?" I asked.

"We'll make sure he doesn't plan on being a foster parent again. And maybe there's a few more things he's up to that don't sit right with me."

"Watch out for the dogs," Davey said. "Most of them just bark, but there's a pit bull called Bruno that acts like he wants to bite just about everybody. But he's just playing. He likes pickled eggs. If you throw him some pickled eggs, he'll leave you alone."

Dad studied Davey curiously. "I'll keep that in mind," he said.

I shook the last of the fuel out of the jerrican and passed it up to Dad. Then I recapped the tank, sat, and pulled the starter cord. After a few tries, the motor fired and rumbled to life.

Davey got in and took his place on the front seat. Then we put on our vests and I began backing us out. Dad remained on the dock until we were motoring toward the river, then waved and started back to his truck.

We passed the fish market where Slade had stolen the money, then the lumberyard where Grover had wrecked his boat. Davey looked from side to side and smiled at his blurry version of the scenery. I thought about him quietly paddling his canoe alone on this same route, just a few weeks before, and how much his life had changed in just that short time.

We pulled up to Grover's dock, and Davey got out and tied the bowline to their cleat like he was proud of knowing what to do.

"*They* got a cleat," he said.

I just shook my head.

Davey followed me up the lawn, gazing over my shoulder, his eyes slowly revealing the full extent of the Middletons' house looming overhead.

"Man," he said.

"He's got his own lair," I said.

"What's that?"

"You'll see."

We entered through the sitting room, and Davey followed me into Grover's deserted playroom.

"Wow," he said, gazing around.

"Yeah," I said. "Big-screen television and about every video game there is. Refrigerator and microwave."

"Pool table," Davey said.

"He's got lots more, but it's all put away right now."

"He must be a millionaire," Davey said.

"His dad probably is," I said, moving toward the stairs. "Come on."

I reached the top of the stairs and entered the hallway. I heard a vacuum running a few rooms away and guessed it was Natalia cleaning. Otherwise the house seemed its usual empty self. I went to Grover's room and found the door open, with him sitting in the middle of the floor with his shirt off and his back to us. He was going through a picture album with the one arm that wasn't in a cast. His torso was still bandaged.

"Hey," I said.

He turned to me like he already knew I was there.

"Hey," he said.

"This is Davey."

Davey lifted a finger at him. "Hey, Grover," he said.

Grover looked him over. "Hey, Davey. How'd y'all get here?"

"My boat," I said. "We found it."

I saw his Xbox sitting on the floor beside his bed and connected to a small television on his dresser. Then I studied the picture album he'd been flipping through. It looked like pictures of him when he was little, standing with his parents. He had the same fuzzy red hair, like a clown doll. He saw me looking and shut the book. I could tell something wasn't quite right about him. I thought he'd be more excited and have more questions for us.

"Help me up, will you?" he said.

Davey and I approached him, and helped him up. Once he was standing he said we could let him go.

"Can you walk?"

"Yeah," he said. "I can walk. It's just getting up and down that's hard. Y'all wanna go downstairs?"

"If you can make it. You thinking about moving down there again?" I asked.

Grover began scuffling toward the door. "Thinking about it," he said. "Come on. I've got something to tell you."

"We can't stay long," I said. "Mom's taking us to get Davey new glasses."

"It's important," he said.

Davey and I followed Grover as he slowly made his way downstairs into his lair. He sat on the sofa and pointed to the two beanbag chairs against the wall across from him.

"Sit on that," I told Davey. "They're real comfortable."

Davey fell back onto the beanbag chair, and I could tell he liked it. I sat on the other one, and then we were looking at Grover, waiting to hear whatever he had to tell us.

"My parents are getting a divorce," he said.

Grover's statement wasn't what I expected.

"When?" I said.

"I don't know exactly when it's official, but Mom came home last night and gave Dad all the paperwork. I tried to message you, but you didn't answer."

"Sorry," I said. "Davey and I went to sleep right after we were texting you about the camp."

"It doesn't matter," Grover said. "I guess I saw it coming."

"So what happens now?" I was suddenly worried that he'd tell me he was moving away.

Grover shrugged. "I don't know. They both came into my room separately and talked to me. Mom says she's already got an apartment in town. She said she's looking for a house."

"So you're moving?"

"I'll probably be going to wherever Mom ends up living, every other week or something like that. I don't think Dad plans on moving anywhere."

"That's good," I said, relieved. "I mean, that you won't be totally gone."

"I guess the thing is, I'm just ready for everything to change. Even if my parents' getting divorced is part of it."

"I felt like that, too," Davey said. "At first I wanted to be with Slade and my dad. And I didn't know how else it could be. Then I realized that I'd just made it all what I wanted in my head. And that maybe it was best that it was going to be another way."

"It may sound weird," Grover said, "but maybe if we have two homes, then I'll see my parents more. I think the reason they're never here is because they just don't want to be around each other."

"You've got to start getting out more, Grover. You can't just sit in here all the time."

"I know. I tried."

"Well, you can't just blow up and spaz out like that. I'll teach you how to drive the *Bream Chaser*."

"I'm just ready for things to be different."

"I know," I said. "And they are. For all of us. It's going to be good."

Grover nodded, still considering everything.

"I'll bet we can use my dad's boat," Grover said. "He wouldn't even notice."

I shook my head and stood. "We're not talking about any of that until you're better. Davey and I have to get back."

I walked over to the big-screen television, grabbed the remote control and the game controllers, brought them back, and set them on the sofa beside him.

"You're just going to have to stay down here and be old Grover for a little longer. When your arm and ribs get better, you can be new Grover."

"When are you coming back?"

"Both of you guys are always asking me when I'm coming back. I always come back, don't I? I'm sure I'll be over here like a thousand more times. And you can always get on your bike and ride over to my house when you get well."

Grover frowned again. "Okay," he said.

"Come on, Davey."

"Check your Xbox messages," Grover called after us.

"Fine," I said over my shoulder.

When we got back to the house Mom was still at work. We made plates from last night's leftovers and were eating them on the dock when we heard the back door shut and saw her walking toward us. She said she'd already talked to two couples who wanted to come see Davey the next day.

"That was quick," I said.

"The social committee has a waiting list," she explained. "A lot of them are people who haven't yet been a fit for one reason or another."

The people none of the kids wanted to live with, I thought to myself.

"The process can take a long time," Mom said to Davey. "Don't get discouraged if these first two families don't feel right to you."

"Okay," Davey said.

That afternoon Mom and I took Davey to the optometrist to get a prescription for new glasses. Once the doctor tested his vision he spoke to Mom about Davey's condition and told her what Davey already knew. His eyes were damaged in a way that wasn't completely correctable, but the glasses would help some. After leaving the optometrist, we went to Walmart and ordered Davey a new set of glasses and got him some clothes that fit him better. When he tried the glasses on and looked at me, it reminded me of our time in the swamp and how he'd always looked and would always stay in my memory.

"You're a handsome young man, Davey," Mom told him.

"You think they'll like me tomorrow?" he said.

She put her hand on his head and rubbed his hair. "I don't think you have anything to worry about," she said.

46

FRIDAY MORNING THE FIRST COUPLE CAME BY THE house to meet Davey. The man was tall and thin and looked like he didn't get a lot of sleep. He was manager of an Auto-Zone in Ocean Springs. His wife was short and plump and worked as a receptionist at the hospital in Biloxi. They had a daughter in high school.

We all went into the living room, where Davey and Mom and I sat on the sofa and the couple sat in the wingback chairs across from us. Mom had told us that she already knew a lot about them from their application, but she asked them questions anyway. Things like where they were originally from and if they'd been married before or had any children from other relationships. The man was soft-spoken and seemed to prefer that his wife do most of the talking. After a moment the woman got a quizzical look on her face.

"Haven't we listed all of this on the paperwork?" she said.

"Most of it you have," Mom replied. "But I'd like Davey to hear it for himself, so we're going to go over some of it again."

The woman raised her eyebrows.

"Is there a problem with that?" Mom asked firmly.

The woman's eyebrows lowered. "No," she said. "Not at all."

"Very well," Mom continued. "Moving on . . . Tell us how often you go on vacation and what your ideal family vacation is."

I couldn't remember being prouder of Mom than at that moment, looking out for Davey. But as the couple continued to talk about themselves and their life, it was hard to tell what Davey was thinking. He sat straight and leaned a little bit forward and listened intently with no expression.

After Mom was finished she allowed the couple to ask their own questions.

"What do you like to do, Davey?" the woman asked.

"Fish," he said.

The wife glanced at her husband, and he nodded agreeably.

"Okay," the woman said. "What kind of family are you looking for?"

"I don't know," Davey said. "I don't know all the types yet."

The woman smiled politely, but I detected a little frustration.

"Is there anything you think we should know about you, Davey?"

"I'm pretty good at makin' things," he said. "And sometimes I have a lot of questions."

"Well," the woman continued, "you can ask us anything you like."

Davey nodded.

"Go ahead, Davey," Mom said.

"Do you have a dog?"

"Yes," the woman said. "We have a dog. A border collie."

"Does he live inside or outside?"

"He lives inside."

"What do you feed him?"

The woman glanced at her husband. "Well," she said, "we feed him dog food mostly. Sometimes table scraps."

"What kind of dog food?"

She looked at her husband again. "Uh, honey, what kind is it?"

"Purina, I think," he said.

Davey studied him. "Okay," he said.

We waited for Davey to ask another question, but he didn't.

"Anything else, Davey?" Mom said.

Davey shook his head. "No," he said. "That's all."

Mom thanked the couple for stopping by, and they got up to leave. Mom told us to wait while she walked with them out to their car. Davey stayed sitting on the sofa while I got up and looked out the window.

"They drive a Honda Accord," I said.

Davey didn't answer me. I turned back and looked at him. He was watching me, but I could tell his mind was going over the interview.

"Honda Accord's not too bad," I said.

"No," he said. "That's not too bad."

After a few minutes Mom returned and joined us in the living room. "Well," she said, "what'd you think, Davey?"

"They seem pretty nice," he said. "When do you find out if they like me?"

"They said you're welcome to stay with them for a few days and try things out if you want."

"So they like me?"

"Yes," Mom said. "They like you."

Davey looked at the floor, thinking to himself again. After a moment he looked up. "But I can talk to some more people first?"

"Certainly," Mom said. "As many as you like. There's another couple who want to meet you this afternoon."

"Then I want to talk to some more people first," Davey said.

"I think that's a good idea," Mom said.

Davey and I went swimming in the bayou, then took the *Bream Chaser* for a short ride. When we got back Mom brought hot dogs out on the dock for us. Then Davey went inside to take a shower and get cleaned up for his second interview.

Davey waited on the sofa while I watched out the window for the new couple to arrive. A little before two o'clock I saw them pull into the driveway.

"Mercedes," I called out. "Jackpot."

Mom came hurrying out of her bedroom and set her lipstick on the kitchen counter. She looked at me and shook her head. "Sam," she said, "get away from the window and go wait with Davey."

I frowned and went into the living room.

"That's not too bad," he said.

I plopped down next to him. "Are you kidding?" I said. "That's as good as it gets."

This time the man was older, with gray hair, and was dressed like a person who played golf a lot. His wife, a little younger than Mom, had long blond hair that hung in a ponytail down her back. She was dressed like she played tennis.

It turned out that he owned a chain of mattress stores around the state, and it sounded like they had a lot of money.

The man asked Davey about his schooling. Davey told him he was homeschooled, and the couple exchanged looks like it was something they weren't expecting.

Then they asked him if he had any medical issues they should be aware of.

"I don't get sick much," he said.

"Do you like to play any sports?" the man asked.

"I like to fish," Davey said.

"He means like athletic sports," the woman said.

"Everything I see is blurry," Davey said. "Even with glasses."

The man studied Davey closely and nodded. The woman leaned back in her chair and rubbed her ear and glanced at her husband.

"What are you interested in studying?" the man continued.

"I like just about anything," Davey said.

"What would you like to be when you grow up?"

"A fisherman, I guess. Or a policeman."

The man sat back and folded his hands in his lap.

"Davey, would you like to ask them some questions now?" Mom said.

"Do you have a dog?"

"She has a wiener dog," the man said.

"Does he live inside or outside?"

The man glanced at his wife. "It lives in our bed most of the time," he said. And he said it like it was a joke, but I could tell he wasn't really joking.

The woman frowned. "Our dog's name is Buttercup," she said. "She's the sweetest dog you'll ever meet. And she has her own bed in the study."

The man looked at Mom. "In *my* study," he added.

"She uses the house just like she's family," the woman continued. "And Bill loves Buttercup."

Davey was studying the man. "Do you love Buttercup?" he asked.

The man rolled his eyes. "Sure," he said. "I love Buttercup."

Davey continued to study him. After a moment he said he didn't have any more questions. Then they thanked us, and Mom walked them out to the car.

"You don't like them, do you?" I said.

Davey shook his head.

I stood up. "Me neither," I said. "You wanna go check on Grover?"

"Yeah," he said.

That afternoon we hung out with Grover for a couple of hours. Then we came back to find Dad getting his boat ready for our fishing trip the next morning. He'd already gone to the bait shop and purchased live shrimp and poured them into the bait well. We helped him put new line on the reels and sort out the tackle box. Then we loaded the fish box, the dining fly, and the foldout chairs and table. Finally we filled a cooler with water and soft drinks and sandwiches Mom had made for us. We iced it all down and got everything ready to leave before sunup.

Back in the house, Mom had a surprise for Davey—she'd picked up his new glasses from Walmart. He slipped them on and grinned at us, and the old Davey was back.

In the evening Dad grilled hamburgers for us in the front yard. Then we swam and tried to catch fireflies with our hands. That night we lay in bed talking about what it would be like living with each of the two couples. I thought the first couple seemed pretty boring, but I wasn't sure what Davey thought about them, so I let him tell me.

"They should know more about their dog," he said.

"Like what? They just weren't sure what kind of food it was."

"They should know," he said. "They should know what he likes to eat."

"They probably do," I said. "It was just a sort of weird question they probably weren't expecting."

"Your mom would know right away what *you* like to eat."

"But I'm her son," I said.

"They should know," Davey said.

And I could tell that I wasn't going to convince him otherwise.

"Everybody's not going to have dogs," I said. "We don't have a dog."

"I know," he said. "But if they have one, they should know all about it."

"Whatever." I sighed. "It's *your* family."

Davey turned on his side and looked at me. "You think I'm bein' too picky?"

"No," I said. "It's whatever you want . . . I just didn't know you cared so much about dogs."

"I told you I did."

"I know," I said.

"The second people with the Mercedes didn't like me."

"How do you know that?" I said.

"I just do."

"Well, you didn't like them either."

"What if I don't find anybody?" Davey said.

"Then I guess you'll just end up living here."

I looked over at him and smiled, thinking he'd like that idea. But Davey wasn't smiling.

"That won't really work," he said.

"It could," I said.

"No," he said. "If your parents wanted to adopt me, they'd have already said so."

"It's not that they don't want to," I said. "It's just not something they've thought about. It's sort of a big thing. It's not like adopting a dog."

"It's okay," Davey said. "I get it."

"It doesn't mean they don't like you."

"It's okay," Davey said again. "I just said that wrong."

"I can talk to them about it."

"No," Davey said. "It wouldn't be right. I need to find my own family. We can still be friends."

"Of course," I said. "Of course we'll still be friends."

Davey smiled and turned over again.

47

DAD WOKE US AT FIVE. HE MUST HAVE BEEN UP
forever, because he already had a breakfast of flapjacks and
bacon waiting for us. Mom came down to say goodbye. She
leaned against the counter in her nightgown and watched the
three of us eat. Dad hurried through his pancakes, taking big
bites and chasing them with milk. Then he set his fork down,
scooted his chair back, and looked at our plates.

"Roger," Mom said quietly, "let them finish."

He looked at her and showed his palms.

Mom rolled her eyes and turned back toward the bedroom.

"It's good," Davey said.

I knew Dad was twitching to get on the water, so I stuffed
the last bite down, drank the last of my milk, and stood.
While Davey finished, Dad and I got the kitchen cleaned up.

"I'll start untying the boat," I said.

"Go ahead and warm up the engine while you're at it,"
Dad said.

I walked out into the damp night. Small birds were making

sleepy chirping sounds. There was a faint glow behind the trees in the east. The bayou was black and still as a lake. As I walked out on the dock I was more excited about Davey seeing the Gulf of Mexico than the fishing trip itself. We hadn't talked about it, but I imagined he'd never seen such big water and open horizon.

I untied the mooring lines and started the motor and stood behind the wheel watching the exhaust float over the water and the engine race rudely against the sleepy dawn. After a moment I heard Dad and Davey coming out of the house. Davey was taking his time, grinning to himself with an air of wonder, and I knew he had no sense of Dad's eagerness. But Dad appeared to be more at ease now, walking behind him with his hands in his pockets. When they finally arrived Davey stood above me looking into the boat like he didn't know what he should do. Dad put his hand on his shoulder.

"Go ahead," Dad said to him. "Let's all get snapped into flotation vests and see what the morning brings."

As Dad raced out the bayou and into the river, Davey and I stood on either side of the console with the damp air whipping our hair back. Davey looked over at me a couple of times; it was too windy and loud to talk, but I knew what he was thinking.

We zoomed under the dark shadow of the I-10 bridge, our

engine echoing loudly. Then the noise was absorbed again by the broad delta marsh as we continued downriver toward the Gulf. After we'd gone another mile Dad slowed the boat. I saw we were before the marine police dock, with Officer Stockton's patrol boat floating quietly in front of it. I turned back to Dad.

"Officer Stockton told me he's been so busy trying to undo what you boys stirred up that he never got a chance to check on you," Dad explained. "He said it's been a while since he's taken a day off."

I looked back at the dock and saw a man walking around the side of the building in the yellow glow of the security lights. He was carrying two fishing rods and a small cooler. It took me a moment to recognize Officer Stockton in shorts, a T-shirt, and a baseball cap.

"He's coming with us?" I said.

"Sure," Dad said. "Why not?"

Dad nudged the boat against the dock and took the fishing rods and cooler from him.

"Morning, Jim," he said.

"Morning, Roger. Appreciate you boys letting me come along."

"We're glad to have the company," Dad replied.

I glanced at Davey. He wasn't wearing his usual smile. He was studying Officer Stockton like the man made him nervous.

We stowed the rods and the small cooler as Officer Stockton

stepped into the boat. Then he held out his hand to me and Davey to shake.

"Good to see you boys again," he said.

I met his firm grip, then watched as Davey did the same.

"Davey," he continued, "you feeling okay?"

Davey nodded suspiciously. "Yes, sir. I'm feeling fine."

"Chest sore?"

"A little bit," Davey said. "Not too bad."

"Everybody get settled," Dad said. "We've got to get out to the islands before we miss that morning bite."

Officer Stockton sat in the seat in front of the console and took his cap off and held it in his lap. I noticed how much more relaxed he seemed than when he was working, or even when he'd been over at our house for supper.

Dad wasn't relaxed at all. I could tell he was antsy again about beating the sunrise to whatever fishing spot he'd probably had in his head all week. He backed away from the dock and pushed the throttle forward, and the boat lunged toward the Gulf again.

The eastern sky was glowing soft pink when we raced out of the Pascagoula River into the Gulf of Mexico. Even if my eyes had been closed, I would have known where we were by the sudden heavy smell of the wet salt air and the boat gently rising and falling over smooth, wide swells. Seagulls dotted the sky, gliding and diving and making their distinctive cries. Miles out I saw Petit Bois and Horn Islands, the water breaking in sharp white lines against their shores. I looked over at Davey, but he kept his eyes ahead, taking it all in like something he'd needed.

The sun was just over the trees in a cloudless sky when we arrived at the south end of Horn. Dad motored to where the incoming tide was curling around the tip of a long finger of sandbar. He slowed the boat by facing up-current while Officer Stockton set the anchor. The seagulls were louder here, swarms of them diving around us along with brown pelicans and sandpipers. We got out our fishing rods, and I showed Davey how to hook a live shrimp through the tail. Before long, all of us but Officer Stockton had our lines drifting out in the blue water.

"Bait up, Jim," Dad said to him.

"Y'all get the first round," he said. "Somebody's got to be ready with the landing net."

"Come on," Dad insisted. "We can figure it out."

Officer Stockton smiled. "I'm fine," he said. "I like watching people catch fish as much as I like catching them."

Dad was about to say something else when his rod suddenly jerked in his hands.

"Fish on!" he shouted.

Then my rod jerked. Then Davey staggered forward and yelled, "Hey! I think I got one!"

The speckled trout came through in waves. Suddenly our poles would be yanked down one after the other, and the boat would turn to mass chaos as we struggled to get the fish to the boat and Officer Stockton dashed about landing them for us. Then there would be a lull of five or ten minutes and then the same again. Davey was beside himself like this was all something he couldn't believe.

As I was leaning back, fighting against my third trout, I glanced at Davey and saw him with the rod handle between his legs, cranking the reel with all his strength. I laughed at the sight.

"Davey!" I shouted.

"W-what?" he stammered.

"Better than catfish jugs, isn't it?"

"This is the best thing I've ever done!" he shouted.

We landed twenty-five trout that morning, some of them as large as five pounds. Officer Stockton even caught two himself after Dad insisted he relinquish his job with the net. By nine o'clock Davey and I were exhausted.

Dad beached the boat and let us get out to explore while he and Officer Stockton wade-fished. Not far up the white sands we entered the cool shade of the pines and started crossing the island on a faint trail zigzagging through the underbrush.

Eventually we came to the wreck of an old sailboat that had likely been washed ashore by Hurricane Katrina. We spent a while exploring the hull and looking for anything valuable. We found a torn life raft and a first-aid kit that was full of water, but nothing worth taking with us. Then we sat on the deck and discussed the possibility of dragging it out of the trees and fixing it up. And after a while we talked ourselves out of it and dropped to the ground again and continued on.

After about a half mile we emerged from the trees and climbed a high dune to look west over the Gulf. Except for a pod of dolphins there appeared to be nothing but blue water and smooth, heavy swells clear to the horizon. Then I pointed out the sinister black fish gliding close to the beach.

"Sharks," I said.

Davey shielded his eyes with his hand and looked where I was pointing.

"You see them?" I said.

He nodded, but didn't answer me. I realized even with his new glasses he didn't see them at all.

"I hope whoever I live with likes to fish," he said.

"You can ask about that," I said. "You can ask about more than dogs."

"And I hope they'll take me places like this," he said.

"You can ask them what kinds of trips they go on."

"I think my dad would have taken me out here," he said.

I wasn't sure how to answer that. "Probably so," I said.

"Maybe," he said, still searching for the sharks.

Standing there with Davey on the deserted island made me think about our time in the swamp again. The two of us alone, with the rest of the world seeming so far away. And for some reason I thought this was the last time it would ever be like that. A lot of bad things had happened that I didn't want to think about, but parts of it I never wanted to forget.

"I see 'em," Davey said quietly, almost to himself, his eyes having found the sharks.

There was something scary about moving on, like walking into a dark room. At least we knew what was behind us. Neither of us knew what lay ahead.

Davey turned and looked at the trees. "You ready to go back?" he said.

"Okay," I said.

48

WE SLID DOWN THE DUNE AND ENTERED THE trees again. When we got back to the boat Dad and Officer Stockton had just finished setting up the dining fly. While we were gone they'd caught five more trout and two redfish.

"I don't think we can hold any more," Dad joked.

"You certainly put us on the fish today, Roger," Officer Stockton said.

Dad shrugged and tried to act modest, but it was obvious he was pleased with himself.

Davey and I helped unload the food coolers, four stadium chairs, and the foldout table. We toted it all beneath the dining fly and set it up. Then we seated ourselves around the table while Dad got out the sandwiches and drinks. He appeared more relaxed now that the fishing was over.

Officer Stockton leaned back in his chair, opened the small cooler beside him, and removed his own sandwich and two honey buns.

"Save it, Jim," Dad said. "We've got plenty."

"Janet got up early and made it for me," he said. "I better eat it."

"Suit yourself," Dad said.

Officer Stockton slid the honey buns across the table toward me and Davey. "There you go, boys," he said. "Looks like she put something in there for you, too."

"Thanks," Davey said, reaching for his.

"Yeah, thanks," I said.

Dad set sandwiches and two Cokes before us. I'd already torn into my honey bun and taken a bite.

"Don't tell your mother you started with dessert," Dad joked.

"What goes on at the fishing camp stays at the fishing camp, right, Roger?" said Officer Stockton.

"That's right," Dad replied. "That's rule number one. And when it comes to meals at the fishing camp, there are no rules."

Officer Stockton chuckled to himself. I noticed Davey was still struggling with the wrapper on his honey bun. Officer Stockton noticed, too. He leaned forward, reached across the table, and lifted Davey's glasses from his face. He looked them over, then took his shirttail and began wiping the lenses. Davey stopped what he was doing and watched him and waited. Officer Stockton finished cleaning and held them up and inspected them against the light. Satisfied, he leaned back across the table and placed the glasses on Davey's face.

"Try now," Officer Stockton said.

Davey looked down at his honey bun, pinched both sides of the plastic wrapper, and pulled it open.

"There you go," Officer Stockton said.

Davey nodded, appearing a little embarrassed.

"I used to carry a handkerchief around with me," Officer Stockton said. "I'd get out in the boat, and my glasses would fog up on me all the time. Eventually I had to start wearing contacts. But they're even more of a pain."

Davey took a bite of his honey bun and chewed and studied Officer Stockton. He swallowed.

"But you do what you've got to do, don't you, Davey?"

"Yes, sir," Davey said.

I noticed how Davey began watching Officer Stockton after the incident with the glasses. And it made me think of the way he looked at him when we were all at the police dock that morning. Only now, it was a more intense look. Like he'd figured something out that made him even more curious about the man.

"I invented a piece of string to keep 'em on," Davey said.

"Yep, that's a problem, too."

"You can use fishin' line," Davey said. "You can't hardly see it."

"I imagine you're pretty resourceful, staying out in the swamp like you did."

"I invented a way to catch catfish, too," Davey said.

"He was good at it," I said. "He tied fishing line to jugs and let them float in the creek."

"I used to dream of living in the woods when I was a kid," Dad said.

"Didn't we all," Officer Stockton said. "But only you have actually done it, Davey."

"It's harder than you think," Davey said. "It gets lonely. I was glad when Sam came to see me."

"Yes," Officer Stockton said, "I imagine you were."

I finished the last of the honey bun and reached for my sandwich.

"What will happen to the camp?" Davey said.

"Parks and Wildlife will probably take it down," Officer Stockton said. "It's not safe to have those things out there."

Davey nodded to himself. I thought about the jugs he'd left arranged neatly against the back wall. Baldy's pot. The old grill and the rusty fork. And I wondered about Davey's canoe.

"What happened to the canoe?" I said.

"We've got it at the station," Officer Stockton said.

"It's stolen, isn't it?" Davey said.

"We're not sure."

"It used to be ours, but I think Dad sold it to our neighbor a long time ago. Then Slade must have stolen it."

"That's good to know," Dad said. "We'll look into it."

Davey finished his honey bun and sat back in his chair. He seemed more interested in Officer Stockton than in his sandwich.

"What do you do with things you find that people don't want?" Davey asked.

"If we can't locate the owner, we'll keep them. Sometimes we auction things off as a fund-raiser. Why? You want that canoe?"

"I just wondered," Davey said.

"Even if we do find the owner, he might be willing to let it go."

Davey nodded.

"You better get something in your stomach besides a honey bun," Officer Stockton said.

Davey glanced at his sandwich. Then he looked back at Officer Stockton. "I've got another question," he said.

Officer Stockton glanced at Dad. Dad smiled at him.

"Go ahead," Officer Stockton said.

"Do you have a dog?"

I stopped chewing and looked at Davey. It was suddenly clear what had been going on in his head ever since Officer Stockton had stepped into the boat with us.

"No, " Officer Stockton said. "I don't."

Davey kept staring at him.

"But I used to," Officer Stockton continued. "His name was Jex. He died last year."

"How?"

"Old age."

"What kind was he?"

"I don't know for sure, but I think a mix between a retriever and a collie. He wandered up to my hunting camp without a collar. I guess he'd been living in the woods. I gave him a piece of my sandwich, and things just sort of went from there. I wasn't able to find his owner."

"And you had him a long time?"

"Yes." Officer Stockton nodded and seemed to be remembering something. "We did. I found him when I was still single. Then I married Janet and he was our family dog."

"Did she like him?"

"Of course."

"Did the dog live inside or outside?"

"He lived outside. He never was much for staying in the house. Sometimes he'd want to come in if the weather was too cold, but mostly he liked to roam around."

"What kind of sandwich made him like you?"

Officer Stockton grinned either at the question or in surprise that he could remember. "Peanut butter and jelly," he said.

"He liked peanut butter and jelly?"

Officer Stockton chuckled. "He liked just about anything, but especially corned beef."

"Some dogs don't like corned beef," Davey said. "They don't like pickled stuff."

"Well," Officer Stockton continued. "I promise you Jex did."

"I believe you," Davey said. "I've known some that did."

"I take it you like dogs?"

Davey nodded.

"I've been thinking about getting another one," Officer Stockton said. "But you know, it's got to be the right one. I mean, it's a big commitment. Jex was with us for nearly fifteen years."

"I'm pretty good at pickin' 'em out."

"I'm not so sure *I* am," Officer Stockton said. "Jex sort of picked me."

"They'll do that sometimes," Davey said. "That's the best kind. They know about people."

"Maybe you'd like to come with me and help me get another one."

"I'd like that," Davey said. "Like today?"

I held my breath. Officer Stockton grinned and looked at Dad.

"Lordy," he said. "You people sure do know how to make the most of a Saturday."

"We have to go somewhere that I can pet the dog," Davey continued. "I can't just look at it through a fence."

Dad chuckled at the odd turn of events. I could tell he knew what Davey was up to. "Ought to be back home in about an hour, Jim," he said. "And Davey's schedule is pretty free these days."

"All right, son," Officer Stockton said. "Let's make it happen."

Davey looked over at me and smiled.

49

DAVEY, WITH HIS STRANGE WAY OF CHOOSING A family, was right to sense that Officer Stockton might offer him the home he was looking for. They left us that afternoon after the fishing trip and went to the animal shelter, where Davey picked out a dog, a mix between a black Lab and a beagle.

They ended up taking the dog to Officer Stockton's house, and to our surprise Officer Stockton called later to talk to Mom about Davey staying the night. The next afternoon Mrs. Stockton dropped Davey back at our house. She was about Mom's size, pretty with short brown hair, and full of energy. Like Davey, she seemed the kind of person who could easily dissolve Officer Stockton's serious side and make him laugh.

I showed Davey the newspaper article in the Sunday paper. He studied the headline.

Boy Leads Authorities to Missing Person and Major Drug Bust

He looked up at me without reading the rest. But no one knew the story better than he did.

"You're a hero now," he said.

"They didn't print our names," I said. "Just Slade's and his friends'."

"Why not?"

"Dad says it's for our safety."

"Oh," Davey said.

"I used to think it would be cool to get my name in the paper, but for some reason I don't care now." Davey and I went out onto the dock, slipped into the water, and floated there, holding the steps of the ladder.

"I think they like me," he said.

"I would have never thought about Officer Stockton," I said.

"Me neither," he said. "But I can tell. I can tell they'll be a good family."

"Did they ask you if you wanted to live with them?"

"No," Davey said. "I told Mr. Stockton that I wanted to."

"What? You just told him?"

Davey grinned mischievously and nodded.

"What'd he say?"

"He said he'd have to talk to Mrs. Stockton and think about it."

"Geez," I said.

"Sometimes you just have to tell people what you think," Davey said, like he suddenly knew all of the answers in life.

"Yeah," I said, still shocked at his boldness. "I guess so."

Davey went back to their house that evening. And again every night for a week. As it turned out, the Stocktons hadn't ever considered adopting a kid or even being foster parents before Davey had suggested it to them. Mom explained the adoption process, and it wasn't long before she was helping them with the paperwork. And Davey had a new home.

After the autopsy was done on Davey's dad, the coroner reported his death as a heart attack. We all went to a small graveside service, where the minister from our church said a few words and blessed the coffin. All the while Officer Stockton stood behind Davey with his hands on his shoulders. Davey didn't cry, but I saw him watching them lower his father into the ground like it was the end of a lot of things he wanted to forget.

Even after Davey moved in with the Stocktons he came by most days and occasionally spent the night. Mrs. Stockton registered him at our school, and though he was going to be a grade behind me and Grover, it was exciting to know we'd be in the same place.

Late one afternoon, a couple of weeks before school started, Mrs. Stockton dropped him off at my house and he proudly showed me his new fishing rod and tackle box. He said that

Officer Stockton had offered to pick us up at my dock and take us back out to Horn Island the following morning.

"Grover can come, too," he said.

"All right," I said. "We'll call him and see if he's up for it."

I called the Middletons' house from the kitchen with Davey watching me. Much to my surprise, Grover agreed to come along like it was something he'd been thinking about for weeks and resolved himself to do.

I gave Davey a nod, and he grinned and clasped his hands together.

"Okay," I told Grover. "We'll pick you up just before daylight."

There was silence at the other end of the line. "Daylight?" he said.

"Yep," I said. "That's when the fish bite."

"Uhhh . . ."

"Gotta go," I said. "Meet us at the end of your dock."

And I hung up the phone.

"He didn't like that, did he?" Davey said.

"No," I said with a laugh. "But he'll be glad about it tomorrow."

Davey was so excited about the trip that he talked me into pitching Dad's tent at the end of the dock so that we could practice fishing that night, camp next to the bayou, and be ready as soon as Officer Stockton arrived in the morning.

We spent more time that evening sitting on the dock looking through Davey's tackle box than fishing. Officer Stockton had taken him to Avery's Tackle and let him pick out the lures he wanted. Davey admired and explained each of them and organized and reorganized them. Eventually we crawled inside the tent with our flashlights. We lay on top of sleeping bags with the night sounds pressing in on us, and I was reminded again of our days together in the swamp.

"When I get to your school I want to see the girl," Davey said.

"What girl?" I said. But I knew who he was talking about.

"I don't remember her name. The one you think is pretty."

"Oh, her," I said. "Julia."

"You just have to tell her what you think," Davey said.

I grinned and shook my head. "You act like you know everything now. You're starting to remind me of Grover."

"I know *some* things," Davey said like he had a secret.

"Just because you used a dog to trick Officer Stockton into letting you live with him. And now you've got some cool marine police dad."

Davey smiled smugly. "It wasn't a trick," he said.

"You picked that dog out for yourself, didn't you?"

Davey shrugged.

"Whatever," I said.

"So you just have to tell her," he said.

"I hardly even know her," I said. "What am I going to tell her?"

"Tell her you think she's pretty."

"Like *you'd* do that."

"I would."

I laughed. "You probably would."

"But she'd like you," he said. "You're the coolest person I know."

The more I thought about Julia's face—the way she'd looked while Leroy and Gooch were beating on Grover and me—the clearer it became just what that look was all about. It was a look of horror and disbelief that people like them existed among us. In that moment, we were all witness to the dark truth that no matter where you are, how safe you feel, there are sometimes bad people looking for an opportunity to do bad things. And it's not all about winning against them; it's about being brave and not losing against yourself.

"Sam?"

"What?" I said.

"I don't know if I can sleep."

"Just try," I said.

"I think tomorrow's going to be the best day of my life."

GOFISH

WATT KEY

© Ward Faulk

When did you realize you wanted to be a writer?

I wrote my first story when I was ten. It was about a collie surviving a tornado. I was into Jim Kjelgaard, a writer of dog books, then, and I wanted to try and make stories like his. I kept writing short stories for fun throughout the rest of my prep school days. My high school creative writing teacher convinced me that I had talent as an author and this gave me the idea that maybe I was meant to be a writer. It wasn't until my sophomore year in college that I knew this for certain. I was running the outdoor skills department at a boys' camp in Texas. I was alone and far away from home, with lots of free time in a little cabin by the Guadalupe River. I wrote my first novel there. Although it was a terrible book that will never be published, it was the most satisfying thing I'd ever done. After that summer, I continued to write a novel a year without regard to whether it would be published or not. I'd written ten novels by the time *Alabama Moon* sold.

What was your worst subject in school?

I remember making an 88 out of 100 on just about every test I took in high school, regardless of the subject. So I wasn't an outstanding student, but neither was I a poor one. At my school, 88 was about average. Before I went to college, my parents took me to see a psychologist in New Orleans. I went through a series of aptitude tests that were supposed to help us decide what profession I was best suited for. Basically, I scored an 88 on everything. The conclusion was that I would always have a hard time deciding what I wanted to be because none of my abilities seemed to stand out above the rest. This didn't help me directly, but ever since then, I've been conscious of the fact that I need to specialize in one thing to be outstanding at anything. For example, as much as I would like to play a musical instrument, I don't. I shun it like a bad vice. I know I would enjoy it too much and it would take away from my focus on being the best writer I can be.

What was your first job?

My brothers and sisters and I always had chores assigned to us that we didn't get paid for. My first duties were emptying the wastebaskets around the house, feeding various pets (we had lots of animals), and raking and mowing the lawn. I landed my first paying job when I was about eight years old. I was the fly killer for the snack bar at a resort not far from my home. I killed them with a washcloth, stored them in a paper cup, and received ten cents per fly. As soon as I would get enough dimes, I would cash in my pay for a drink to quench my thirst.

How did you celebrate publishing your first book?

My wife and I went to the Mexican restaurant up the street. It was a fairly low-key celebration. It took a while for me to accept that I'd gotten a legitimate book deal. You may have seen the episode of *The Waltons* when John-Boy gets scammed by the vanity publisher. He told all of his friends and family that he'd gotten a book deal and they had a big celebration for him. Then he got a letter from the publisher asking him how many of his books he wanted to pay them to print. It was a scam. This exact thing happened to me years before I sold *Alabama Moon* and it was very embarrassing and eye-opening.

Where do you write your books?
After college, I built a small camp several miles into the swamp that you can only get to by boat. I made it from lumber that washed up on the beach after a hurricane. It took me nearly every weekend for a year to complete it. I develop and outline most of my ideas up there. The bulk of my actual writing is done at home in a spare bedroom that doubles as my study.

Where do you find inspiration for your writing?
I'm not always inspired to write. Fortunately, I have a backlog of stories in my head that I feel have to be written whether I'm in the mood for it or not. I often tell people that writing is like an addiction to me. I liken this addiction to people who jog every day. I don't feel good about myself unless I'm doing it. Most of the time, it's a very enjoyable process. Sometimes, it's not. But I decided long ago that I was supposed to be a writer, so that's what I do.

What sparked your imagination for *Hideout*?
I've always carried a strange fascination with abandoned cabins deep in the wilderness. I think about the articles left inside them—old toys and fishing rods and candles and pots and pans—and I imagine who was last using them and what they were thinking. And I wonder what the circumstances were that led them to leave a place where they spent so much time and made so many memories. I thought it would be interesting to have a boy find such a place and try to fix it up and live in it with limited resources. So I came up with Sam

and sent him out into the swamp. Originally I was going to make Davey a ghost, but ultimately decided against it.

Are there parallels to your own childhood in the story?
I had a boat around the time I was Sam's age and it was about the same size. From the moment I got that boat I was overcome with a sense of freedom and adventure. Just about every time Mom's car left the driveway, my gas can was in the back of it needing a refill.

What was your favorite scene to write?
My favorite scenes always end up being the ones that were easiest to write. I think this is because I visualize them so well that I feel like I'm there and not really making anything up. In the case of *Hideout*, it was when the boys were lost in the swamp, wading and swimming through the dark floodwater with only the sound of a distant owl to guide them. I know the uneasy feeling of swimming in the darkness without any real idea of where you are. And I know how terrified I would be of the alligators and snakes lurking in such a place.

How did you decide what kind of dog Davey would pick out for Officer Stockton?
That one came to me easily. I got it right in the first draft. I figured Davey would pick a dog that he thought no one else would pick just to give it a chance at a good home. Like the chance he was given by Officer Stockton.

Where did you come up with the name of Sam's boat, the *Bream Chaser*?
I know a fellow whose citizens band radio handle is Bream Chaser and I've always thought that was a great CB name. But on a different level I saw Sam's dad as a bit overshadowing

and imagined that his naming Sam's boat after a tiny fish might contribute to Sam's struggle with self-esteem issues.

In the book, Sam contemplates if his good intentions justify the lies he tells, and later Davey tells Sam, "Sometimes you can lie if it helps people." Do you agree with Davey?
While I firmly believe there is nothing worse than a liar, I think it is okay to occasionally lie in a selfless way in order to save someone pain or grief. That's not being a "liar."

When you finish a book, who reads it first?
My wife, Katie, reads my first drafts most of the time. I've learned that if I don't want her to read it, it's probably not ready. Then my agent reads it, and finally my editor.

Are you a morning person or a night owl?
I'm a night owl. But to feel good and productive, I have to have eight hours of sleep, no more, no less. I usually write from about eight until eleven at night and get up at seven in the morning.

What's your idea of the best meal ever?
Rib eye steak. Egg noodles with real butter and garlic. Real mashed potatoes without gravy. Cream cheese spinach. Brewed iced tea with lemon, real sugar, and mint. Lemon pie without the meringue for dessert.

Where do you go for peace and quiet?
My swamp camp.

What makes you laugh out loud?
Mark Twain.

What do you value most in your friends?
Honesty. Originality.

What is your favorite TV show?

I don't recommend television. One day I was driving through Mississippi and came across a folk artist with a yard full of his scrap iron creations. Out front was a sign that read "Look what I did while you were watching TV." I like his attitude.

What's the best advice you have ever received about writing?

Continue to write even when you don't feel like it. If you're a real writer, that's what you have to do. I knew this on an instinctive level for many years, but never heard it described as well as what a painter friend of mine told me. I was watching him create an oil painting of an outdoor scene. He was doing his work in a small, rocking boat, crouched beneath an umbrella in the pouring rain. I remarked that he was the most dedicated artist I'd ever met. He responded by telling me that he wasn't an artist, he was a professional painter.

When her father falls ill, it's up to twelve-year-old Julie Sims to lead two of his clients on a scuba dive. But when things go unexpectedly awry, can Julie keep her divers safe from threats of hypothermia, shark attacks—and worse?

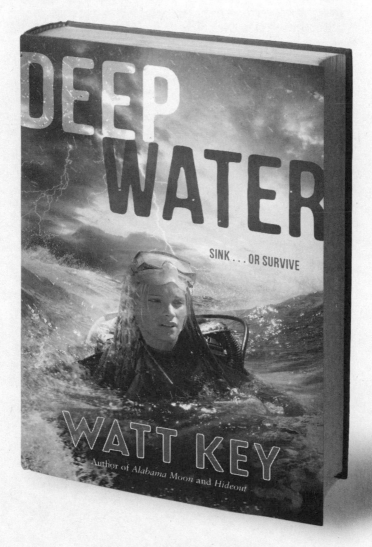

Keep reading for an excerpt.

1

THE GPS BEEPED, SIGNALING OUR ARRIVAL AT THE DIVE SITE. DAD slowed our old twenty-nine-foot trawler, the *Barbie Doll*, and I sat up and peered through the windows of the wheelhouse. We'd lost sight of land over an hour ago. Nearly thirty miles off the coast of Gulf Shores, Alabama, there was nothing to see above the waterline except for an endless expanse of swells shimmering in the sunlight. But off our port side I saw a swarm of fish descending in a column through the jade-colored water.

"You're right," I said to him. "There's fish all over it."

Somewhere in the depths below were two army tanks, government surplus from the Vietnam War. Three years before, my dad, Gibson Sims, had been hired to tow them out on a barge and push them into the water, where they sank to the seafloor to create an artificial fish habitat. Then, through an unfortunate occurrence that had nothing to do with him, the coordinates were lost and the tanks presumably abandoned forever beneath over a hundred feet of water.

It wasn't until a week ago that Dad found the tanks again. He said they'd attracted barnacles and tiny fish, which in turn attracted larger fish until the tanks were a fully developed reef. Now the reef was home to hundreds of varieties of fish and resembled an amusement park for sea creatures.

I was eager to see the reef, but most important to me that day was knowing these tanks could save Dad's charter business. We needed to make sure our clients, Hank Jordan and his son, Shane, had a good dive and told others about it.

"Yep," Dad said under his breath, "they'll get their money's worth."

I sensed he was nervous, too. He knew as well as I did how important this dive was.

I looked at him. He was barefoot in his swim trunks and a faded madras plaid shirt. His wild gray hair seemed permanently stiff with dried salty water. His face was a little sunburned, but he was still fresh and youthful-looking, like a boy trapped in a middle-aged body. He was a big bear of a man, but he often reminded me of an overgrown kid. And despite the family and financial problems we'd left ashore, I felt proud of him for the first time in a long while.

Just the anticipation of a scuba dive can melt your worries away. And once you descend into the blue-green depths it seems the rest of the world doesn't even exist. I feel like an astronaut drifting in silent, immense space. Only this space is not dark and empty, but full of colorful sea life. Nothing compares to the thrill and peacefulness of hanging weightlessly in this mysterious world of exotic creatures.

Dad glanced behind us, making sure our clients were still seated on the back deck. The location of the tanks was a valuable secret, and he didn't trust them to keep their eyes off our navigation equipment. Those two were about as difficult as they came. Both Mr. Jordan and Shane spoke to us rudely, didn't listen to advice, and were always arguing with each other. Dad was still stewing over Mr. Jordan insulting his charter operation that morning and looking down on me like a twelve-year-old girl had no place on the boat. Normally he would have told them to take their business elsewhere, but today they were paying nearly four times our usual rate—and we needed the money.

"I don't think they can see the GPS from back there," I assured him.

Dad frowned doubtfully and wiped his forehead again with a hand towel.

"How do you feel?" I asked.

On the way out I'd noticed him sweating and wiping his face. I guessed it was his diabetes and got him a candy bar, but he didn't seem any better.

"Dad?" I said again.

He didn't like talking about his health and didn't seem concerned about it either. I felt like I was constantly having to monitor him. I recalled a dive the summer before when we'd had to surface early because his blood sugar was low and he got disoriented at fifty feet. It was episodes like that which worried me.

"Dad, are you able to go down or not?"

It was over a hundred feet to the seafloor, and I wasn't a certified dive master like he was. I'd certainly been that deep many times before, but it wouldn't look very professional to the Jordans if I replaced Dad as their guide. But if something were to happen to Dad at those depths, people like the Jordans couldn't be relied on to help him.

"Mr. Jordan won't like me guiding them," I said.

"I'm not worried about what that jerk likes and doesn't like," Dad replied. "Those two are reckless enough to get themselves in trouble down there. And I don't want you mixed up in it."

"I can handle myself," I said.

"I know . . . But I can still be worried about it."

Dad's the toughest person I know. I once saw him stitch a cut on his leg with a fishhook and fishing line so he wouldn't have to end a dive trip early. I knew if he decided to send me in his place he would have to be feeling really bad. But one of the most important rules of diving is if you don't feel right, don't go down. There are already too many things that can go wrong with a person's body in the depths without adding other complications.

I exited the wheelhouse to find the Jordans arguing about their spearguns and who got to take the larger one. Shane was about my age. He and I had been in the same class at elementary school when I lived with my parents in Gulf Shores. That was before Mom and Dad divorced and I moved to Atlanta with Mom, leaving Dad behind in our old house. Now Shane was taller than I remembered, and he'd grown his hair out so that it hung almost to his shoulders in a style popular with local surfers. He wore a Salt Life T-shirt, AFTCO shorts, and deck sandals, all of it looking like he'd pulled the price tags off that morning. He's smart, athletic, wealthy, and good-looking if you like the type. I don't like the type.

Even when we were younger, he struck me as one of

those kids who complain about everything like they're in a constant battle with an unfair world when I can't imagine they know anything about unfair.

Shane's father was a local attorney, but his face was on interstate billboards clear to Montgomery. On the advertisements Hank Jordan looked tall and young in a trim, expensive pinstripe suit. He held a stern expression and had his arms crossed over his chest like he'd just solved a big problem. What I saw standing before me in a fishing shirt, shorts, and Crocs was a shorter, wrinkled version of the man on the signs. He looked a lot more like an aging weasel.

"This it?" Mr. Jordan asked.

"Yes," I replied as I made my way up to the bow. "We're at the Malzon tanks."

That's what Dad and I called them, after the guy who hired us to put them in the water.

I unfastened the anchor chain and held it while Dad maneuvered the *Barbie Doll*, taking it in and out of gear and assessing the current. Finally I heard him tap on the window glass. I let the chain slip from my hands and heard the anchor plunge into the water. For scuba divers this basic piece of boating equipment is much more than something to keep us moored in place—it's our guide to the seafloor and our lifeline back to the boat. I leaned over the railing and watched the white rope stream into the depths. The visibility was decent, but the current was strong up top. I hoped it wasn't as swift down below. That's one problem with scuba diving. You don't really know what dangers you're up against until you're deep into them.